NEBERON COMES

SUZY VIVIAN

SWEETSPIRE LITERATURE
—— MANAGEMENT ——

CONTENTS

PROLOGUE

I N BOOK TWO, The Mist Monsters, our friends, Jasmine, Donavan, Zarcon, Greta, and Magg were able to spend some time recovering from their adventures with the witches' coven headed by Zora with Anesthia, Myshella, Heleren, and her sister, Magg. They had destroyed the Blue Orb and the witches but their journey was haunted with many perils as they traveled to rid the world of the Blue Orb.

One of the worst things they faced were the monsters in the mist. Once they were able to rest in Synkana, they decided that those monsters were to be their next mission;; to end the terror they had been causing in the land.

In the meantime, Magg, the sister of Zora, had been left at home in the witch's castle. She had been a disappointment to her sister, Zora, so she was not allowed to go with the witches to retrieve the Blue Orb. Magg felt rejected because of that, but in the long run, she was actually grateful she had not gone with them. She never really felt part of the coven. Her heart was soft and she loved animals and some of the people she knew. She was teased by the other witches mercilessly as a result.

She found out awhile later from one of the villagers that her sister and the other three witches of their coven had failed in their quest to get the Blue Orb back. Later, she found out that the witches had either been killed or hanged. Much to Magg's surprise, she didn't feel sad at all. In fact, she was relieved. Zora had been so evil all her life and now Magg was free from her. Now her life was her own and she could find a way to learn about her own magic. She thought that if she could find Zarcon, maybe he would teach her what she wanted to know about magic that would help others. She was hoping he would let her join his group and learn good magic so she could make a difference in the world and make up for some of the evil Zora had done to so many.

Zarcon and his friends wanted to celebrate the wedding of Jasmine and Donavan. It was a much needed diversion from all they had faced recently. Now they could help plan and enjoy some happy times along with resting from all they had suffered. This included the deaths of so many of their friends. It was a good time to heal and recover.

Magg was finally able to find Zarcon and his group of friends and join them just as they were leaving Synkana. She had a gypsy wagon and was able to be of help to Zarcon in traveling to destroy the monsters. As she worked with Zarcon, she found out in course of time that she did indeed have very powerful magic and was able to save the lives of many people.

Echeron and Lucain were two young men from the small village of Anakik who were also seeking Zarcon's help. The monsters in the mist were terrorizing their village and they had been sent to find Zarcon and enlist his aid. They also arrived in Synkana just as Zarcon's group of friends were leaving to begin their mission to eliminate the monsters. This was fortunate because now Zarcon and his friends knew where to begin their journey to destroy them.

So the group plus three new friends were on their way to Anakik to begin helping the villagers there. When they finally got to the village, there were more monsters than they could have imagined. In fact, they seemed able to multiply and have some kind of intelligence as a group. Unfortunately, some of them had migrated to the next village. So now the group was divided. Some are helping those in Anakik and others are helping those in the nearby village. This was not a good time to have the group divided.

~

There is an evil presence by the name of Neberon coming to destroy all those with magic, and maybe even the whole world. He was wakened by the magic used to destroy his precious mist monsters. He knows the magic used is powerful, yet he firmly believes that he has more powerful form of magic. He is dark and difficult to define. He is not quite human, but more in a form of evil. He rides a black horse that has the same undefined form. He is very angry. When he passes, he is not seen, mostly felt. Babies cry, dogs howl, and adults feel a chill up their spine and terror in their hearts.

He is coming…

CHAPTER 1

A GROUP DIVIDED

As our group of friends, Zarcon, Greta, Jasmine, Donavan, and Magg and the others in their group are fighting the mist monsters, their feelings of dread begin to grow. Greta in particular is feeling what's coming. The name of the evil is not known at this point, but the fear and dread grow as Neberon approaches.

Unfortunately, the group is divided. Magg and Donavan are in the village not far from Anakik finishing the fight with the mist monsters. It has been a desperate fight with many villagers injured and a few deaths. Magg has learned much about healing and restoring health. Her magic is becoming so much stronger in that regard. The magic takes a toll on her strength, however, because it is very powerful magic. But she is determined to help all she can.

Donavan is also learning how to calm and heal the villagers. He also has very strong magic and is also getting stronger. Jasmine has joined him, bandaging and following the directions from Magg and Donavan on how to help. They are working well as a team. The villagers are more than grateful for their efforts. So many lives were saved as a result of the magic used.

Finally, the work is close to completion and all that could be helped have been. Magg, Donavan, and Jasmine are ready to rest and head back to Anakik.

The remaining members have been in Anakik rebuilding the village after it was nearly destroyed by the Black Wind. There was still work to be done and the village inn was being rebuilt and supplied with the things that were destroyed by that wind. The villagers from the nearby village have donated things needed for the inn in exchange for their help in destroying the mist monsters for them. So, all that was left to do was to put it all right for the inn. And their work was nearly complete.

The Black Wind had struck the village to destroy those who were associated with calling it forth to destroy Zarcon's castle by the witches led by Zora and her sister witches. The witches were gone, but the Wind came to exact revenge on Zarcon's group regardless of who really called it. Zarcon had been concerned about the possibility since his castle was destroyed. He knew that the Black Wind wasn't called forth without some kind of consequence that would not be good. It could not be known how the Wind would exact revenge until it happened.

Now Greta has become increasingly ill from her feelings of dread of the evil that she has felt since they began their journey to Anakik to help the people fight the monsters. Zarcon has become more and more concerned for her health. She has been eating less and less and can't sleep.

Zarcon finally lays next to Greta to comfort her and hopefully give her strength to go on. "Greta, I have loved you for so long. You are my life and my joy. Please don't leave me now when things are getting so difficult with the evil that's coming. I don't think I can fight it without you near me."

Greta sighs, "Zarcon, I have loved you, too. I love your strength and kindness. You have kept me going all this time. Now I feel like it is time for me to leave. I'm too ill from worry and the sense of what's coming. When the time comes, please let me go."

Zarcon couldn't help himself, he started to cry softly at the thought that she was thinking of dying even now. Zarcon now regrets that they never married, though they have loved each other dearly. So, with her being near death, Zarcon is almost frantic to help her get her health back. The problem is, it's not of this world and he has no control. He doesn't know enough about it. He only knows that it is killing his beloved Greta. Greta is an empath and is very sensitive to such things as this evil that approaches. That is why she is so ill and is nearing death.

Zarcon has felt some of those same feelings of dread, but for him, it's not so strong. He can still take care of the things required of him, but he is living in a world of worry and dread for what he might be able to do without Donavan and Magg. He fears that if the evil comes before they return to Anakik, he won't survive the fight alone. He is feeling his age and some loss of his powers as a result. Any fight with a power as great as seems to be heading their way will probably be more than he can overcome alone.

~

Meanwhile, Donavan and Magg are feeling the need to get back to Anakik and find out how things are going for Greta and Zarcon. Both of them have had the feeling that they must get back to help Zarcon fight whatever it is that is headed their way. They were hoping they could get back in time. The only thing they know for sure is that what is coming is very evil and extremely powerful.

While fighting the mist monsters, Magg found a new spell that she had been unaware of until she started helping Zarcon's group destroy them. She was even able to teach her new spell to Donavan and Zarcon. Magg's help resulted in the monsters being destroyed at a much faster pace than they could do before.

More of the villagers were saved as a result of her efforts and those of Zarcon and Donavan. Without her spell, the monsters may very well have won the battle and possibly been a threat to the survival of all life in this world. Magg has been feeling the power of magic in her life like never before. Donavan has noticed her increasing power and has felt his own power growing. It is such a great time for both of them to be coming into their own.

CHAPTER 2

NEBERON MOVES OUT

THE BEING NEBERON is coming to destroy all those with magic who have been killing his precious mist monsters. They have also scattered his Black Wind. He does not forgive. He is enraged and seeking revenge. His eyes are the indicators of his wrath. They are deep blood red. They shine forth from him, lighting the area around him. His cloak hides what is left of his body. He has been so long in his cave that a lot of his body is part of the cave rock itself. It was difficult for him to separate his body from the cave after sleeping there so long. So by now his body has become partially flesh and partially stone. This is his weakness. Movement is difficult when he is not on his horse.

His image is difficult to determine. He is black as night and the edges of his cloak seem to swirl and shift in such a way that it appears that he has no distinct edges. He is a fearsome creature that sends out feelings of fear and dread by simply moving out of his cave with the intent of doing harm. He has stepped on the ledge of his cave to survey the world below. He can sense the magic there and senses one who is more powerful than the rest. This one he fears but refuses to admit it.

Neberon decided to leave his cave and called his horse, Negra, to him. This is such a new experience for Neberon and he is excited to see what the world holds for him. As he and Negra step over the lip of the cave, they send out the message that evil of an intensity never before seen is now on the way to cause destruction and death.

Neberon is moving through the world upon his horse, Negra. Negra is more spirit than flesh. He is solid black and blends with the night. He also seems to have no edges but is blurred by his lack of physical substance. He trails a strange vapor as he passes. To inhale this vapor is to die a quick and painful death. The two of them make a deadly pair ready to destroy all others with magic, especially those involved in killing his mist monsters and scattering his Black Wind. His eyes shine forth in a deep blood red. His gaze is penetrating and can kill when the victim is alone.

Neberon decided it would be of benefit to himself to practice his power on a few villages before he reaches his objects of revenge. He has searched the area ahead and finds a small village, Maldorn. It looks quiet and humble. It is exactly the place he would like to start his practice of magic. He can sense a bit of magic here that makes his idea even more enticing. No one expects his attack, which makes it more exciting to have the element of surprise. He's feeling the need to warmup for the time when he reaches those who are harming his precious mist monsters.

He can't bear the thought that someone could kill them. He had created the current monster to be able to multiply and to have some intelligence. He was excited to see what kind of damage they could do with such power. Now, he would probably never really know. It infuriated him.

As Neberon approaches the village, he has decided to start by using one of his favorite spells to destroy the wall surrounding this village. As he casts the spell, the wall starts to crumble to dust with a great crash. The people of the village are now aware that a great power is present.

They have started by gathering up the children and running for safety. Neberon will not allow that. He must destroy all before they can mount any defenses. For him, destruction is its own reward. He will happily ruin this small village just for the joy of doing so. In fact, the villagers' screams excite him like he has not felt in many eons.

The people are starting to run for the forest. He has very little time now to make his move and start his next favorite spell. He raises his arms and says the words of his spell. Red light flashes between his upraised hands. He conjures the spell and throws his glowing red ball of power toward the largest group of people trying to escape him.

The ball of power hit the ground near the middle of the group and shattered like a large glass vase. The occult pieces hit the group like a missile and cut off body parts and killed most of the people with pieces of the spell embedded in their bodies. There is poison in each shard of the red glass. When hit, the person usually died within a short time.

The others kept running for the forest. Though most of them were injured, they were able to make it to the edge of the forest before another similar spell was cast in their direction. The second spell killed the rest of them before they reached safety.

Neberon was truly enjoying himself as he had not done in so many long centuries in his cave. He was wishing in his twisted mind that he had done this long ago. He'd forgotten how rewarding it could be for him to destroy life. Now, he remembered and knew that was what he was meant to do.

~

The villagers that had gone the other way to escape Neberon were able to just barely do so. They made it to the next village and warned them of the coming evil that had killed so many of their village. Panic set in immediately and the people took whatever was at hand and left their village in haste. The forest seemed to be the only place they could hide in any safety. So that is where they ran.

One of the men, Adrian, a town leader, led the way to a part of the forest that had numerous caves and dens. He told the villagers, "Please check inside the cave to make sure there are no wild animals waiting to attack you. This area is known to have many large animals that are very dangerous."

It could be very dangerous for the unwary or stupid. In fact, one family decided it was a waste of time to check and ran into a likely cave only to find a large black werecat living there. This werecat is special. It can change shape as needed. This cat used to belong to a man by the name of Black Hawk. After he was killed, the cat ran away and wasn't seen again.

Needless to say, it didn't go well for them. The cat was especially ferocious and the screams and growling in that cave caused the rest of the villagers to go see if they could help. Only one of the older, more cautious, boys, Zolar, survived by not going in with the rest of his family. He almost ran into the cave to try to help. He could see that anything he could try to do would be worthless and result in his own death as well. So, he hid in the brush not far from the cave and waited to see what would happen.

When the screaming stopped, the cat ran out of the cave with blood all over its jaws and paws. It looked around and finally jumped across the trail and disappeared into the forest. It was never seen in this area again. Where it went, no one could say.

Zolar was devastated by the loss of his family. He felt their loss and was deep in grief. But he had learned a valuable life lesson. It was better to be cautious than to rush in with high hopes and fail or worse, die. He decided to join the last group of villagers looking for a cave to hide in. They welcomed him and gave him a blanket and what little food they could share. He would be alright for now.

It didn't take long for most of the villagers to get into the caves. They moved as far back into the caves as they could and reminded each other to be very quiet. Adrian made sure all the people were settled before he finally joined his own family in the second cave. He was hoping the evil one would be gone by nightfall and move off. Maybe with any luck, at least some of them would survive. He had a very bad feeling about this. He had never even heard of the spell that other villagers told him about that killed so many. It was a terrible thing. He knew it wouldn't be long before this great evil would come looking for them. It was a difficult task of waiting for that to happen. All he could do was pray to the gods that some really would survive.

~

Now that Neberon had increased his appetite for destruction and murder, he moved on to the next village. As he approached the village, he sensed that the people were gone from their homes and other areas in the village. He felt a momentary sinking that maybe he wouldn't be able to have any pleasure here. It was a dreadful feeling for him since he had enjoyed destroying the previous village so much.

Fortunately for Neberon, he remembered another power he had and that was one he used rarely, but it worked wonderfully well. He could cast a spell that would amplify his hearing to a great extent. It was useful but also potentially dangerous to him. If he heard a loud enough noise while in that spell, it could damage his brain, what little he had left.

So, not hearing any noises from this village, he decided to use his spell. He dared not use it for long, only long enough to try to hear the people and where they might be. Nothing happened for a few moments, then suddenly, he heard a soft baby cry coming from the hills inside the forest boundary. His excuse for a heart leapt for joy, he had them now. An evil grin spread across his face and his eyes were a softer red. The smile felt very strange on his face. It was a very nasty expression on a face like his. The atmosphere of evil increased. It spread to the villagers in the hills. They all suddenly felt very cold and the babies started crying and could not be comforted. Now, they knew death was coming.

Neberon was now on the move toward those hills in the forest. He urged Negra forward. They moved smoothly together barely touching the ground. They followed the obvious trail left by the villagers as they headed for the caves. Neberon burst out laughing at how stupid they had been to leave such an obvious trail.

The sound of his laughter was like the scream of a strange animal that went on and on. It was bone chilling. This was heard for miles around. The good thing was that it alerted the other villages nearby that something was not right in the world. The cold chill of evil was stronger than ever and people could feel it was very close. The feeling had been vague before, but now it was becoming almost painful for those nearby. Some of them were vomiting in the grass. Others had raging headaches with no relief. Dogs whimpered and cried. Children clung to their parents for comfort. But there was no comfort.

Neberon decided to take his time this time. He could see that the fear that was building would make his actions even more terrifying. So, Neberon and Negra approached the area of the caves. He could smell the fear. It excited him all the more. He knew this was going to be one of his favorite moments since leaving his cave.

8

The villagers in the caves could hear the soft clip clop of Negra's hooves coming closer and closer. They went as far back into their caves as possible, hoping to delay the inevitable. There was no weapon devised that could save them now. It was magic coming for them and not one of the villagers had any training or experience in it. So, wives clung to husbands and children clung to their parents. All were weeping softly.

As Neberon approached the nearest cave, he decided to try a spell he hadn't used in a long time. It was very painful and provided a slow and painful death. He began his spell, waving his arms and chanting the spell. He directed the spell into the first cave.

Suddenly, there was some very loud screaming and crying as the spell took effect. This spell was meant to melt the bones of any it was directed toward. It was indeed a slow process and extremely painful. That's why it was one of his favorites. The screaming was so rewarding to him.

While the first cave of villagers were dying, Neberon moved on to the next one. These people were even more terrified with the sounds of those in the first cave's screams. They spoke together for a few minutes and agreed that they would rather have a sudden death than what was happening to the others. So, they decided to rush whatever monster came to them and hope that he would end their lives quickly. They could see no other option.

Neberon approached the next cave with a red gleam in his eye. He was hoping for more of the same reaction to his spell. Just as he got to the cave, the villagers ran at him screaming and throwing rocks. One lucky shot hit Neberon on the head. This so infuriated Neberon that he cast a fire spell and incinerated them all at once. He was so shocked by their actions that he was stunned for a moment or two. He could not guess at why they would do such a thing. He decided that he must be more careful from here on. So, he approached the last cave with some caution. He now knew that the people were smarter than he had previously expected.

The people in the last cave had heard all the screaming from the first cave and decided that waiting for death in a cave might not be the best option. The cave they were in was large enough for many of the villagers. Their cave was around a bend in the mountain trail, out of sight of Neberon. So as soon as the screaming started, they decided to leave the cave and head up the mountain to find a safer place to stay.

One of the villagers, Osherman, knew of a place higher up where there was a lake and lots of trees and underbrush to hide in. He also knew that the terrain leveled out not far ahead. The going would be much easier if they could just get there before they were discovered to be gone from their cave. They left very quietly, carrying the children and keeping them quiet as well. They knew that their lives depended on getting as far away from what was happening as possible. Courage gave them strength to keep going and fear spurred them on. When the land started to level off a bit, hope began to rise in their hearts. Maybe they had a chance to survive this after all.

Neberon was not pleased that he had been forced to burn all those villagers. He had wanted to torture them before they died. The previous cave had been very satisfactory. He could still hear some of them screaming in pain. Only a few left now.

What Neberon did not know was that in the very back of the second cave, two small children remained. They were so afraid that they huddled in a small corner of the cave in a slight bend in the back of it and made no noise. The flames didn't reach them, just the heat. Their hair was singed a bit was all that happened to them. They had survived the attack.

So it was that these two brave children were all that remained alive of those in the cave with them. They stayed there in the cave long enough to be assured that the monster was gone from their village. They were eight and ten years old and very smart to be able to survive such an attack and to not follow their families into death. Now, they were alone and afraid, but alive. They would spend many years suffering from all they had seen and heard that terrible day. Even so, they were grateful for the choice they had made to survive. Their names were Kedron and Boren.

Neberon decided to wait awhile before he would go to the last cave. The use of all that magic, especially the fire, had taken a toll on his strength. It was then that he realized he was indeed affected by the amount of magic he used in a short period of time. But this was something he could not accept. The reality was that he needed to rest before taking on any more magic. This was fortunate for the villagers in the last cave.

So, he rode Negra to a quiet part of the forest and rested, "Just for a moment or two." He was able to rest while being on Negra. He knew the people of the next cave would wait in fear for him to "take care of them". He was also sure that the longer it took him to go to the cave, the more the fear would overtake them and make them easier to torture. He would start with the children. That had always created the fear and hatred in others that he loved. Oh yes, this would be exciting indeed. He just needed a bit of a rest. He had not realized that his magic could drain him to such a degree. He started thinking about that aspect. In the back of his mind, he wondered if part of him was human or some other lower creature. He was supposed to be an immortal. Now, a bit of fear crept into his heart. Could he possibly die?

CHAPTER 3

VILLAGERS FIND A SAFE PLACE

OSHERMAN WAS LEADING the villagers from the cave they had been in. As they moved away from the cave, he realized they were leaving a trail that the monster could easily follow. So he told the last families in the group to take tree branches and drag them across the trail to hide it as they moved quickly up the hill. He also asked the group to spread out as much as possible in order to leave even less trail for Neberon to find. The trees were now farther apart with little underbrush.

After walking for some time and since the ground was leveling off, he knew that the area he sought was not far away. The group found new strength and started to run now that it was easier going. They were leaving a very confusing trail now, so covering it was of no use.

Finally, as they rounded an outcropping of rock, they could see the glimmer of the lake not far ahead. The older children started to race to the lake. It was beautiful. The people were so grateful that Osherman had shown them where to go. He was their hero.

The group moved to the opposite side of the lake to find shelter and a place to hide from Neberon. Fortunately, this area was dense forest. They scattered to find their own spaces to hide. They gathered tree limbs and branches around them and some found spaces under pine trees where the limbs were very low to the ground and yet had space close to the trunk of the tree. The needles on the ground provided some cushion from the ground beneath. It would do until they knew they were safe from this evil creature. They could not know whether Neberon would find them or not. The fear was palpable not knowing what would happen to them if he did indeed find them. They only knew it would be terrible.

Now, it was a matter of waiting to see what would happen if Neberon should figure out where they had gone. It surely was hoped that he would give up and move on to some other place. They were afraid that if Neberon did find them, he would be so much angrier for having to go after them. The thought was horrifying. But one thing was also certain, to be free for any amount of time would be worth whatever it cost. These people were brave and strong in their desire to be free of Neberon and his terrors. Only time would tell if they could succeed in escaping his wrath.

～

Meanwhile, Neberon had rested sufficiently to move forward with the destruction of the rest of the villagers. He was feeling so much better after his little rest that he was anxious to start his rampage. He took his time, wanting to draw out the fear of him that the villagers were surely feeling. As he drew closer to the last cave, he noticed that there was no noise coming from within the cave. This made him a bit curious and anxious to find out why.

Neberon rode up to the cave and left Negra to look inside. To his horror, the people were gone! He could not believe such a thing could be possible. The people didn't seem to be smart enough to desire to escape. They could be anywhere. How had they done this without him hearing them leave? As he searched the cave, he became more and more angry.

The villagers would pay for this, oh yes! His anger had reached new heights and it was a level of rage that was dangerous to any and all nearby. His eyes were a deep blood red now. As he left the cave, he sent a blast of power that leveled all the trees and other growth for a mile around. Smoke rose from the power he used that sent a message to any who saw it that trouble was on the way.

He was hoping the message would get to those villagers who had tricked him and left their cave. Either way, he was on his way to find them and make them pay as no other had before. He would find them and they would be punished severely. He could hardly wait!

~

As the villagers waited, they were getting more and more fearful that Neberon would indeed find them. They were concerned that it had been so long since they moved to the lake. They began thinking that maybe Neberon would not come after them and move on to the next place that he could cause mayhem and death. Of course, this was dangerous thinking. It was much too soon to be thinking such thoughts because Neberon was seeking them even now. And it was sure that he would find them sooner or later.

Suddenly, they saw the smoke from the spell Neberon had cast. They knew then that they were in for a really bad time if he found them now. So, they became even quieter as they waited.

Neberon would not allow such treachery to go unpunished. It was a matter of pride and reputation that he did not allow this to go without retribution. As he searched, he was thinking of all the nasty spells he could come up with to use on these people. He had much evil power to play with. It made him smile at the thought. He would make sure they would scream for mercy for a long while before he ended their miserable lives.

CHAPTER 4

GRETA AND ZARCON

Z ARCON WAS INCREASINGLY concerned about his dear friend, Greta. She was failing rapidly and he was feeling the pain of loneliness already. He needed her calming influence and her strength. She gave him such good advice and was very logical. She was also tuned in to spiritual guidance as well. As an empath, she could also influence the emotions of others if needed. She had been invaluable when the Blue Orb had been destroyed. She had influenced the men nearby to go after the witches and destroy them by giving them courage.

It was known by only a few that Zarcon had met Greta many years ago. He was so much younger then and in the height of his power. He was part of an elite group of wizards. He was the most powerful of them all. He seemed to be destined for great things in his life.

Greta was even more beautiful then. He was introduced to her by one of his fellow wizards, Locoran. Zarcon was told that Greta was an empath and might be helpful to him. His interest increased and he sought her company. They spent a lot of time together getting to know each other. Zarcon was becoming more and more convinced that he wanted to have her as his friend.

They walked together in the park nearby and talked while sitting on the bench near the stream that flowed through the middle of the park. It was such a beautiful place and so romantic. Greta saw Zarcon as an amazing wizard who was handsome in an old-fashioned way. He was older but he was also very kind to her. She decided she would like to be his friend. So, as they talked together one afternoon on their walk, they decided that being friends was the thing they wanted most. From that moment on, they were almost inseparable.

Their friendship was very powerful. It was almost like they could read each other's mind. He had learned to depend on Greta for so many things. She helped him in so many ways. He was there for her as well. They helped each other through all of life's ups and downs.

But now, when Greta wasn't doing well, he was feeling very nostalgic and extra affectionate to her. He held her as often as time allowed. Greta told him she was grateful for the comfort he was giving her. She told him to take care of the others. She didn't want him to neglect his duties as leader of the group and village. Zarcon knew Greta was also concerned for everyone else, but it was also true that she didn't realize how sick she really was. It was really difficult for Zarcon to be busy and away from her at this time.

Zarcon was also very concerned that the others had not returned from their work at the other village. He was feeling the evil approaching rapidly and was very much afraid that he would have to face the evil alone. He knew he didn't have the strength to do so. He was fearful of what could happen to the others if he could not fight because of his age and current state of health. He kept praying the others would get back before whatever evil was coming actually arrived.

Zarcon tried to prepare himself mentally and to rest for the coming battle of magic. He knew he wouldn't last very long in such a battle, but he would do all he could to protect everyone until the others arrived. Age had indeed taken a toll on his strength and power. He was still powerful but not as he felt he needed to be. The evil that was coming was terrifyingly strong. He decided to study his history books that he brought with him wherever he went. Maybe he could find out something about this creature.

As he studied, he discovered an old legend about a wizard named Neberon who had left his fellow wizards to try spells that were not approved of by the others. He had turned from the desire to help to the desire to harm and destroy. The legend suggested that he had become very powerful and his passing created fear in any nearby. He had been shunned by the other wizards when he suggested that they could use their powers to rule the world. He had been thrown out of the palace they lived in. Xyrene had been the head wizard at the time and was responsible for his being outcast.

Neberon had traveled the land bringing harm to any and all. He was greatly feared. He also experimented with creating creatures and powers forbidden by the code of magic. He used his creations to further the threat of destruction and death.

As Zarcon read about this Neberon, he realized that it was highly likely that the evil that was threatening them was indeed Neberon. Now he understood what they were likely facing and it terrified him. He would discuss his findings when Donavan, Magg, and Jasmine returned.

Now at least they had some idea of what was coming. Maybe they could make a plan against him. They must or all would be lost.

CHAPTER 5

KEDRON AND BOREN

T HE TWO BOYS, Kedron and Boren, were traveling through the villages away from where the evil creature had been. They would take no chance of meeting him again. As they moved through the land together, they asked other people if they knew of anyone who could help them. They were told more than once to seek out the wizard Zarcon. It was reported that he and his friends had been destroying the mist monsters and were not far away.

So, they decided to find them and see if Zarcon could help them and find shelter with them. Surely those with magic could protect them from the creature that had killed their families. In addition, both of the boys' parents had possessed magic but had lost it due to not using it much over the years. Their quiet village seemed to get along well without it.

Now the boys had a goal to find Zarcon and seek his aid. They were also interested in getting help in deciding if they had magic. If they did, they really wanted to learn more about it and its use. They were excited to see what they could learn. It became very important for them.

They left the village and started off on their own again. One of the families had taken them in, fed them, and let them stay for a few days to rest and recover from their terrible experience. Boren thanked them for their kindness as they left.

The family had also given them long knives to protect themselves as they traveled. The forest and road ahead could hide any number of dangerous creatures, animals as well as humans. Both boys felt better with the knives as protection.

They stayed close together as they moved on. Now, they could see the danger they were likely in on this road alone. Every once in a while, there would see travelers along the way. But the boys ignored them and kept walking. When a large group could be seen in the distance, they moved off the road and sought shelter in the forest. They would watch the group go past and listen to what they were saying. Sometimes, it was frightening. They spoke of the creatures that lived in the forest and what had happened to some of their friends. It kept them alert to anything out of the ordinary.

They began to think that if they had horses, they could make better time. So, they kept alert to a way to get two if they could. Even one horse would be helpful. They had no money, but could work hard. They were thinking maybe they could find a farmer willing to give them a horse or two in exchange for their labor. It seemed like a good idea at the time.

CHAPTER 6

FINALLY BACK TO ANAKIK

A S THE MIST monsters were destroyed and the people of the village were being cared for, the people who were not injured came to Donavan and told him how very grateful they were that this group had come to their rescue. They had been through so much together that it seemed difficult to see them all leave. They were able to help them pack and give them food for the trail ahead. The people told Donavan that any time they were nearby that they could come to their village and they would have a great feast to celebrate.

Donavan was a bit embarrassed by all the attention. Magg and Jasmine were happy that they had been able to help Donavan express those feelings. But now it was time to leave.

The pressure to be going back to the village of Anakik where Zarcon and Greta were trying to get along without their help was growing. Donavan had told Jasmine that he was feeling the need to get back. Both Jasmine and Magg agreed that it was time to be moving on.

With the help of the villagers, they were getting all things ready. The time spent there had been good. They had destroyed the mist monsters that had been plaguing them for so long. Now, it was time to go find out about the evil that was headed their way. Their group bade their friend's goodbye and they wished them well and a safe ride back.

Donavan was glad that they were leaving that morning. It was early yet and there were only a few things to discuss before they left. Donavan spoke to them privately and said, "We must be careful as we travel back to Anakik. Don't forget that there are other dangerous creatures in the forest, even though the mist monsters are gone. We will ride swifly. The need for us to get back to Zarcon and the others is vital now."

Donavan dismissed the group and they were ready to leave in just a few moments. They mounted their horses and were ready to ride. Donavan gave the word and they took off, riding swiftly knowing they were needed elsewhere. Their horses seemed to sense the urgency and were ready to run.

Donavan was in the lead with Jasmine close behind. Magg followed Jasmine, Matton and the others followed them. They were all on hyper-alert status, not sure what they would deal with, if anything, as they hurried back to Anakik.

As they rode, they noticed something moving in the forest that was keeping up with them, but not attacking. Donavan was watching the movement anxiously. Whatever it was seemed to be very large. It was black and hairy with what looked like long teeth. It started making gruff noises that were deep throated and angry. None of the friends had seen anything like it before.

Suddenly, it crashed through the undergrowth and was about to attack Matton. His horse screamed in fear and started to rear and almost threw Matton to the ground.

Magg had prepared herself to use her magic to take care of whatever it was in order to protect the others. She was just in time to send a ball of fire into the beast before it could do any real damage to Matton or his horse.

The beast roared and tried to crawl toward Matton, but died in the effort. Magg and Donavan jumped off their horses to see if Matton was alright and what the beast was. Neither of them had seen one of them nor heard of them before. This was a new concern. One they did not need right now with the worry over the evil on its way to destroy them.

It was huge and could have caused Matton and his horse serious injury or death. If Magg had not been with them, they might have all been killed.

Magg was at Matton's side and making sure he was uninjured. She hugged him and he hugged her back. It had been too close a call for them both. Magg was falling in love with Matton and if anything would have happened to him, she would have been devastated.

"Magg, you saved me! I thought for sure I was going to die. That thing was so big and nasty coming right at me. What in the seven hells was it? Does anyone know?"

"No, I'm afraid we have never heard or seen anything like it either. Donavan, do you know anything about this creature?"

Donavan thought for a moment, "I seem to have heard rumors of such a thing in the past, maybe when I was a child. But I thought it was a story made up to scare me. I couldn't say for sure. Anyway, I think this one is much larger than anything I've heard of."

Magg asked, "What shall we do with it? I could incinerate it. What do you think? We can't take it with us, that's for sure."

The others laughed at the idea. Matton said, "I really like the idea of seeing you incinerate it. It would give me great pleasure to see it gone."

"Alright, here goes..." Magg started chanting and let the power gather in her hands. She threw the ball of magic at the body of the beast and in a few seconds all that was left was a pile of greasy ashes. "I suppose that takes care of that." She brushed her hands together for effect. Matton smiled.

The others applauded Magg. It was gratifying to see the creature gone. They didn't even have to bury it.

So, now they could get going again and head for Anakik in hopes that this creature was the last thing to slow them down or cause anyone of them harm. Fortunately, the rest of the ride was quiet and uneventful. They knew they must report the creature to Zarcon, he would want to be made aware of it.

As they neared Anakik, things seemed different.

CHAPTER 7

NEBERON SEEKS ONE WITH MAGIC

NEBERON WAS TIRED of looking for the villagers who got away. He had no idea which direction they had gone in. He could find no trail, which was odd in itself. There had been a large number of villagers in that last cave. To top it all off, it had started to rain. Now, what trail there might have been was washed away. Neberon hated the rain.

After some time spent looking, he realized the hopelessness of it and he was miserable and wet. The forest was too large for him to search the entire area. Besides, his rage had cooled enough that he decided to move on to more fruitful adventures. He was frustrated and growing impatient with the search. As much as he hated to admit it, he had been outsmarted by a bunch of ordinary people. He had not realized the power of wanting to be free from tyranny and fear. So he decided to stop the search, though it galled him to do so.

He was thinking that it was time to look for anyone who might possess magic and destroy them. That was what had brought him out of his cave in the first place. He was beginning to think that he had actually been wasting his time on those villages. He had enjoyed himself but now he realized it really was a waste of time.

Now that he had made up his mind, he realized again that this would be even more fun because the battle would be much more interesting and challenging to attack someone who could fight back, even if only for a short while. He wanted to start with a person of little magic first to see what would happen when he showed up to fight. He could sense someone several miles away from where he was. So he urged Negra on and they moved forward to follow Neberon's sense of where this person was.

Neberon sensed that the person was young and unused to his craft. This could be risky because a new person has little control over their ability and might be dangerous because of the use of wild magic. Neberon was feeling strong at this moment and knew that no amount of wild magic could beat him. He was, after all, the best wizard known in all the worlds. At least, until he felt one a bit stronger recently. But this was not that person.

He rode toward a village by the name of Solvig and began his search for his next victim (er, opponent).

~

The village of Solvig was very small with only three hundred villagers. Everyone knew everyone else. It was a very close-knit community. The forest was close around them and there were many animals the men could hunt for food. The people had gardens and fruit trees. The houses were painted bright colors and their clothing was beautiful. It was a really quiet place with a few dogs and cats running around to keep them company. The children were taught by their mothers and fathers. They learned about the history of the land and how to read, write, and understand mathematics. The villagers were happy and productive taking care of the important things in life: family, community, and education.

The person Neberon was seeking in Solvig was a young man by the name of Jarrone. He was just finding out how to use his magic. His mother was a very powerful witch in her day, so he wasn't surprised when he discovered his talent. His mother had taught him all she could before she died, which was quite a lot, actually. He had been working on his skills since he had passed into puberty. He still didn't have the control he needed to be really great, but he was improving daily. Neberon could not know this.

Jarrone had learned many spells that would cause an explosion and many that would bring sharp, whirling discs to target. Another of them was very dangerous. He could send a fiery blast of power strong enough to level trees for several yards from where he stood. Those trees then burst into flames so hot that no one could go near for several days. The odd thing was that the fire didn't spread to other trees or buildings. He was excited about this new spell and kept working on it to make it even more specific. He wanted to be able to use it on one specific area or person of danger if needed. He hoped he would never need it, but it would be great for a defensive spell.

He felt the need to be able to protect himself and his family so he mainly worked on defensive spells. Sometimes, his spells came out much bigger than he had anticipated. Once, he blew up the cowshed, completely destroying it. Fortunately, the cows were in the field at the time. But his family was upset with him nonetheless. He quickly helped replace the cowshed.

Jarrone also found that he could bring a small cyclone and use it to pick up things unwanted, such as an old can of paint. He was working on using it to pick up unwanted suitors of his sister. He could pick them up and have them thrown a mile away. They would suffer some injury, but not death. He wanted to make sure they never came back.

It was working great, but Jarrone was not comfortable using it unless the young man was aggressive with his sister. If the person continued after being warned, Jarrone was forced to use the spell to get rid of him. He was glad he had learned that one.

He had two sisters and one brother. Revinia was very beautiful for one so young. Lucintha was very pretty, but not quite as pretty as Revinia. Revinia had long black hair and was very kind to others. Her slender figure attracted most of the eligible young men in the area and beyond.

Lucintha was a few years younger and not ready for courting. She had red, gold hair that she kept short for convenience. She was a very active young girl and wanted to keep her hair out of the way. It was not fashionable for young girls to have short hair, but Lucintha didn't care. She did what she did for her own comfort. Revinia would cut it for her to make sure it looked good enough for public view.

Jarrone's brother was named Hoskins. He was the youngest of the family and tried to help, but usually ended up making more mess than helping. He became a bit rebellious when he was teased about it. He was also a bit hyperactive and was often seen running through the forest chasing whatever animal caught his attention. It was thought that Hoskins could have a bit of magic, but it would take some time for it to appear. It was common for magic to be discovered during puberty. So Hoskins had a few years yet to know for sure. He was only eight at the time.

Jarrone's father was getting old and needed help for many things. His sisters, Revinia and Lucintha, were very good to help him. As a result of their help, Jarrone was able to practice his magic for longer periods of time. He stayed mindful of what was happening in the home throughout the day. He didn't want any surprises. He was taking over many of his father's duties and responsibilities as well. He was the eldest child and felt the weight of those responsibilities.

Add to that the fact that his oldest sister, Revinia, was coming of age and was having suitors call. He was not happy about that and had chased off some of them. He could read a person's character in their face and knew which ones were no good. Just the threat of him using his magic on them was enough to scare most of them off. He watched all the others very carefully. He wanted his sister to be safe and happy as she became a woman. She mostly appreciated his efforts in her behalf. However, there were times when his concern was quite aggravating.

There had been an episode when a handsome young man came courting. He seemed really nice and was kind to Revinia. The problem started when Jarrone sensed that he was not exactly honorable. So he warned the young man to leave Revinia alone. He refused and said he wanted to have her come and live with him in another village quite far away. He neglected to mention marriage.

Jarrone was offended and warned him away once more. When he refused saying he was "in love with Revinia", Jarrone decided to teach him a lesson. He sent a shock spell at him and singed his hair off. The idiot screamed and ran away never to be seen again.

Revinia had been furious at the time, but after talking with Jarrone about what the young man had suggested, she felt better about him being gone. She was still irritated, but not angry.

They were very close as a family and loved each other dearly. They would each do anything to help the other. Their home was cozy and warm in winter with fireplaces upstairs and down. In summer, they could open any of the many windows and get plenty of fresh air. The house was made of field stone and had a thatched roof. It was two stories high with four bedrooms and a loft. The furnishings were of good quality because their mother would have it no other way. She had been making money from her magic and healing spells until her death from a mysterious illness. Their home was really comfortable. They had a wonderful garden in the back near a brook that crossed the property. They were very nearly self-sufficient.

The girls sewed their own clothes and made shirts for Jarrone and their father. They could make amazing dresses from the scraps their mother had left them. All kinds of fabrics were available in a big box in the loft area. It was fun to see what they came up with.

Revinia was especially talented. It was thought that she might have a bit of magic too. She was that creative. Lucintha mostly made the men's shirts. She made them very well, but was not really interested in making the fancy things that her sister made; though she did love to wear them.

So Jarrone was very busy protecting everyone and learning all he could about the magic he possessed. There was much to learn. Yet, he was well on his way to becoming a master wizard at his young age.

One morning, Revinia came to Jarrone and asked him to test her somehow to see if she actually had some magic. She said, "Jarrone, I'm feeling some strange new stirrings that make me feel like magic is coming alive in my life. I've felt it before when I was sewing something new. But now, it is much stronger and I feel the need to get your help. You know so much about magic."

Jarrone thought for a moment and said, "You will need my help to get through entry into real magic. I was lucky because I had mother to guide me. The thing I worry about is you being divided in what you really want now. Young men are paying a lot of attention to you and you will need to figure out what matters most. Have you thought about it much yet?"

"I have given it a lot of thought and I've decided that this magic is the most important thing for me. I can do a lot of good in the world with it.

The young men are just a distraction right now. I certainly don't need that, not like I have felt the need for magic. Will you help me?"

"I'm so glad you feel that way. I've been concerned about the path your life seemed to be taking. And now I need to teach you the valuable lessons I've learned along the way. We'll be in this together. What do you say?"

Revinia smiled, "I'm in it with you as far as this can go. When can we start?"

"How about tomorrow morning?"

~

Neberon had a tough fight on his hands. Fortunately, he was unaware of the danger he was in. Even though he thought he was eternal, it was possible to cause him great harm. Only time would tell if it were true.

Meanwhile, he was moving toward Jarrone's home, hoping to have a quick end to this young person who possessed powerful magic. He wanted to get to him before he became too powerful. The thought that this young man could threaten him was completely ridiculous in his eyes.

So, Neberon kept moving toward Jarrone in hopes of eliminating him before he could become a real threat. The problem was, Jarrone was already a real threat and growing stronger every day.

Revinia was learning quickly. She found that she could use her magic to create illusions of beauty or of terror as she felt the need. Lucintha learned how powerful those new spells could be. She was hanging up some wash one morning when she saw a pretty horse not far from her. When she went to get closer, the horse disappeared. It was just an illusion Revinia had created to see Lucintha's reaction. It was fun. She also knew she could scare people with her other illusions. But she decided she would never do that to her sister.

Revinia would learn much from Jarrone in time. Jarrone was happy to help her. It was great to be able to teach another person about magic. It strengthened his own knowledge and helped him better understand what he already knew. As a result of teaching Revinia, they became even closer as siblings. It was fun to talk together about what they were learning.

Revinia was the creative one. She came up with more ideas of how to make things look a certain way to other's perception. Lucintha was getting a little jealous that the two of them were closer now. But she was glad Revinia had new things to learn and practice. It did leave Lucintha to spend more time taking care of their father. Otherwise, she would have become lonely. So much for them to do and yet Jarrone was concerned about the evil presence he could feel coming their way.

CHAPTER 8

BOREN AND KEDRON FIND A FARMER

B OREN AND KEDRON were looking for a farm that they could possibly work on and help the farmer so they could earn a horse or two with their hard work. The problem was, they were still so young, only eight and ten years old. They didn't stop to think about what they could really do on a farm that would earn a horse or two. This would prove to be a problem.

They came upon a small farm that looked like needed some help. When they came up to the door of the farmhouse, they knocked and waited for an answer. It took a while for the farmer to come to the door. When he finally got there and opened the door, a strange gleam came into his eyes.

Kedron noticed it and was about to run when Boren spoke up, "Hey mister, we'd like to work for you so that we could earn enough to get a horse. We're traveling alone and need a better way to get around than just our feet, if you know what I mean. Do you have any work we could do for you?"

Kedron pulled on Boren's shirt to try to tell him they needed to leave, but he was ignored. Boren was the oldest and thought he should be in charge. Unfortunately, he was not the smarter of the two.

The farmer, Zedoc, was very glad to hear what Boren said. He needed help alright, but not what the young boys were thinking. This man lived alone and he was very lonely. So having these boys show up was just what he wanted. He would keep them with him forever if he could. They wouldn't even need all that much food or care. He had a special place to keep them. It would be so good for him to have their company.

Kedron had increasingly bad feelings about this farmer. He could not believe that Boren had trapped them so easily. He knew they would both be at the mercy of this man. He knew from this man's eyes that he was not a nice person. Now, only time would tell how bad things were going to become.

Zedoc invited them into his house and when they were in, he locked the door. No sense risking them getting away. Kedron began to shake from fright. Boren was oblivious to their danger. He was much too trusting.

Once the boys were inside, they noticed the filthiness of it. It wasn't just dirty, it was plain to see that rats inhabited it as well. Rat droppings were everywhere. Urine stains marked the corners and everywhere near the walls and under the furniture. There was nowhere to step that wasn't disgusting.

Boren finally woke up to their situation. He looked at Kedron in fear. Kedron just shrugged, he didn't know what to say. All was lost now. There would be no escape for them.

Zedoc knew he had them. He said, "Well, here we are, right where I want ya. Let me show ya yer new home." He half-giggled.

He took them to the cellar where he kept a couple of small cages that he was planning on stuffing the boys into. Kedron tried to fight him off, but Zedoc was too strong, and he smelled so bad Kedron couldn't take much of it. So he had to comply to get away from him.

Both boys started to cry the minute Zedoc left the cellar. This was too terrible and they'd only been there a few minutes. If this was any indication of what was coming, they were frightened more than they had been the entire time with Neberon.

What frightened them so much was the unknown of what he would do to them. With Neberon, they knew that whatever he did would be short and terrible. But with Zedoc, they had no idea what he was going to do with or to them.

They cried all night. They were so very uncomfortable and feared what the next morning would bring. They so feared the sound of Zedoc coming down the stairs. They could only hope that he would bring them something to eat that wasn't contaminated.

Kedron finally spoke to Boren, "Didn't you feel me pulling on your coat when we got here? Didn't you notice the farmer's eyes and horrible smile? Why did you have to ask him if we could help him? We should have run away as soon as he opened the door!"

Boren started crying again, "I'm sorry, Kedron, I wasn't thinking and thought I was older and knew better. I was only hoping to get some work so we could get a horse. I didn't think we would meet someone so evil. I'm so sorry I'm not very smart. I don't think ahead very well."

"If we ever get out of here, I will never speak to you again. We'll be lucky to survive this. I'm really afraid."

"So am I. We've got to come up with a plan to escape even if it takes us awhile to do it."

Just then, they could hear Zedoc coming across the floor to come down the stairs to where they were kept.

"Well, well, well, how are my new friends this mornin'? I could hardly wait to come see ya. I'm hopin' ya'll are doin' real well. I woden' want ya to be unhappy now. Ah did bring ya somethin' ta eat. I feed this same stuff to the rats ever day. They're doin' well as I'm sure ya noticed."

"I'll cum bak an' see ya later on. We have lots ta do. I need ta train ya to wut I need ya ta do fer me. Eat hardy me lads." He laughed as he left them to go upstairs.

The boys looked at the so called food Zedoc had left them. It truly was disgusting. They tried to eat it, but after one bit, they both vomited. It tasted of rat crap. But what could they do? No food, no sleep, no escape, and no help for them. No one knew they were there. Their families were gone. Their situation was settling in and they both lost hope.

CHAPTER 9

MAGG AND HER MAGIC

As Donavan and Jasmine, along with the others, entered Anakik, it was obvious that something was very wrong. Some of the villagers came to help them with the horses and their belongings. But no one would talk about what had happened while they were gone. The subject was too raw at this moment.

There seemed to be an air of grieving about the village. Their small group ran toward the place where Zarcon was staying and burst through the door just in time to see Zarcon leaning over Greta with tears in his eyes. He was crying softly. Greta was lying on her bed barely breathing. She was still alive, but for how long? Zarcon was obviously beyond the ability to talk about what had happened.

It was shocking to see Greta, who was much younger than Zarcon, being so close to death. Magg came closer to Zarcon and quietly asked if she could help. Magg was confident that she really could help Greta, if allowed to do so.

Zarcon finally raised his head and looked at Magg. He suddenly realized that his friends were back and able to help. He nodded to Magg and stepped back a pace so Magg could get closer to Greta. She sent a thin tendril of magic into Greta to evaluate what was going on. She found that Greta's heart was laboring and her soul emanated fear which was hard on her heart.

Magg withdrew the magic and told Zarcon what she had found. He told her that he had found the same things, but had not been able to do anything about it. Magg reassured him that she could help. She had a special healing magic that she had been working on during the quiet times while helping get rid of the mist monsters. Those who were injured offered her a place to work on that magic. She was able to heal most all of those she treated except those who were ordained to die.

So, now she was sure of her ability to help Greta. She started by sending magic that would strengthen Greta's heart. It was difficult because Greta was so full of fear. As a result, Magg began to chant a calming spell. She was telling Greta that all would be well. Her friends were there to take care of whatever was making her so afraid.

Gradually, Greta's breathing settled down and her color began to improve. Magg continued to chant to her and then started singing words with real power in them. The sound had a profound effect on Greta. After a while, Greta's eyes fluttered open.

Everyone cheered when they saw that Greta was improving. Greta was startled by all the noise and was surprised at the sight of her friends all around her. Zarcon came closer and sat beside her on the bed. He was smiling in relief and joy to see her so improved. Magg quit singing and just smiled.

Zarcon was overjoyed and gave Magg a big hug of gratitude. Magg told him that Greta would improve slowly and get back to her sweet self, but in the meantime, she needed to be able to rest and recover. That's when the others left her and Zarcon alone. He needed to be with her and spend time with her alone.

Donavan was so curious to know what power Magg had used to cause such a marked improvement in Greta. He knew from observing her that she had been very near death. How could Magg have pulled her back from the brink in so short a time?

"Okay, Magg, we need to talk. What have you learned that you could save Greta like that? She surely was at death's door when we walked in. How did you learn to do that when Zarcon couldn't?"

Magg was embarrassed by the question and thought a minute before she answered. "Donavan, I learned a lot when we were helping those other villagers and all their injuries from the mist monsters. I looked deep into the magic to find new ways of healing. It came to me so fast and I learned much just by asking the right questions.

"Donavan, I think I might have extra magic that I can learn from as I need it. Remember what happened when you were about to be killed by that mist monster? Remember the spell that just came to me to save you and the other people nearby? I taught you and Zarcon what I had learned, right?"

"Right, I remember. It was amazing."

"Well, this is beyond that, and I can see that I will be able to learn even more as I progress. I'm so excited! This is what I've been hoping for since I was a little girl. I've always hoped to use my magic to help people and even save lives if possible. Do you see what this means to me?"

Donavan was quiet for a few minutes, then said, "Magg, what I saw today is beyond anything I've ever seen or heard about. Now, you tell me you can learn more just by digging deeper? I'm so excited to see where you go with this. We do have something evil headed this way. I'm really confident that you are going to be the key to helping us destroy whatever it is."

"Oh, Donavan, I'm so hoping that is true! I know that is what caused Greta to nearly die. She is so full of fear that it was really difficult to calm her. When I had to switch to singing that was an indication of the power that I had to draw on to help her. I'm actually exhausted by it. I really need to go to my room and rest for a bit. We can talk about it some more, later, if that's alright?"

"Of course, Magg. You will be needed later, but I'm sure a few moments of rest are a good idea."

All went to their rooms at the inn. A rest was needed by all those who had been in the other village and the ride back to Anakik had been tiring as well.

~

Zarcon was so relieved that Greta survived that he was once again on the verge of tears. He had been face-to-face with the fear that he might lose Greta. He couldn't bear the thought. She was his best friend and his rock of sanity. She meant much more to him than he had previously realized. Now, it was his job to see that she stayed with him alive and well.

"Greta, I was so fearful that I would lose you. Are you feeling better? I couldn't bear it if you left me."

"Oh, Zarcon, I could feel my spirit ready to leave my body. I know that I would have died without Magg's intervention. She truly is amazing. She brought me back to life and calmed all my fears. I have found that whatever happens with the evil that is coming, I want to be a part of whatever it takes to destroy it. I will not fear it anymore. Fear only makes things worse. I will feel the fear, but not to the extent I have in the past. I let it get into my heart and soul. I can't let that happen again."

Zarcon hugged her for a very long while. It felt so good to both of them that they couldn't bear to part. He loved her more than ever now that he realized he could lose her so quickly. She was his heart.

CHAPTER 10

WHO WILL BE STRONGER?

NEBERON WAS MOVING closer to the little village where Jarrone was living. He was looking forward to taking on this young man of wild magic. He wanted to test his abilities against him. He anticipated that it would be entertaining at the very least.

It may turn out that his pride will cause him problems. He has no idea what he will face and isn't interested in learning any more about Jarrone's magic. We'll see how this turns out.

~

Jarrone is at this moment practicing another spell he has recently read about in his mother's old Book of Magic. It looked difficult, so to Jarrone it was a particular challenge. This was what he loved to do. He could figure out how it worked and make it happen, he was very sure. This particular spell was one that could freeze anything for however long he wanted it to stay frozen. It would be so fun to try it on one particular suitor of Revinia's. He was very persistent and would not leave her alone. This would be the perfect surprise for him next time he came calling. His name was Rolfo and he was short and hairy with a large nose and bowlegs. His belly hung over his pants. He was also an annoying person with little personality. The only important thing to him was Rolfo. He could talk about himself for hours.

Jarrone had made great progress on this spell and was perfecting the timing of it as he imagined what it would be like to see Rolfo's face when he used it on him. As he was working on it, he began to feel something coming that was of intense evil. It was so strong that he went to the house and told his sisters to stay inside and protect their father. Something was coming to hurt them. His sisters started to cry, but Jarrone assured them that he would protect them as best he could. He knew his magic was strong, but was it strong enough?

He went around his small village to warn all his neighbors of what was coming. Many of them said they felt it too. So everyone closed and barred their doors for however long it would take until the evil was gone.

Jarrone was getting anxious. He could sense that whatever was coming was a very powerful and ancient evil. He didn't try to build up false pride. He just went over all the spells he knew and which ones would likely be best for a fight of magic. He was young and far more powerful than even he knew. So, maybe he had a chance against Neberon. Regardless, Neberon was coming.

~

Neberon was on his way to meet this boy wizard and was excited to see what the boy knew. He was hoping there would be more than just killing him. Maybe they would be able to exchange a few spells before Neberon had to kill him. He was also hoping he could eliminate others while he was there. He needed some excitement to get his energy back and killing was one way to replenish it.

He decided he would play a short game of cat and mouse while he was at it. He would start small and build his spells until the boy couldn't compete. Then he would die.

The killings he had done so far were satisfying, but not a challenge. He was hoping meeting this young man would be just that. He would see how strong he was then work his magic accordingly. If he offered any challenge at all, it would be so much more enjoyable.

38

He and Negra rode through the night to get to the village of this young wizard. The night was cold, but he didn't feel it. The creatures anywhere near became very quiet. They knew it would not be good to attract the attention of this evil creature that moved through the night. It kept them alive for another day.

Neberon did enjoy killing small animals just for fun. It helped distract him from his path to the young man he would destroy shortly. As he got closer, he began to have some anxiety about his ability against this young man. He didn't really understand why except that he was possibly much stronger than anticipated.

As he got closer, he knew he must maintain his level of confidence or all would indeed be lost to him. This was no time for questions about his abilities. So he concentrated on building his confidence to a new level. He would not allow any doubt to enter his mind. Doubts could be the death of him.

CHAPTER 11

ZEDOC AND THE BOYS

Things were getting worse by the moment. Kedron was made to scrub the filthy floor. He had no broom to start getting the filth out of the room. Boren was made to clean the kitchen where the rats had the run of the place and made terrible messes all over the counters and table. Both of them had a terrible time gagging and retching as they worked. They only had pails of dirty water to try to clean everything. It ended up that they were just smearing it around. The smell got much worse as a result of getting it wet.

Zedoc came into the room to check on them frequently. He always struck one of the boys and made a terrible remark to them. "Ya'll are stupid if ya can't do a better job of cleaning up the place. Ya'll are just making it smell worse."

Neither of the boys dared say anything. Zedoc had to know why things smelled worse. He seemed to take delight in cruelty and shaming them. It was plain to see that if they said anything, it would go really bad for them.

Day after day was much the same. They were told to clean the same areas even though it was not possible to get any of it clean. Gradually, the boys were getting used to the smell and filth. Their clothing began to smell like the house and their skin was as well. They kept trying to eat the food Zedoc brought them, but they could not and were getting really thin and sickly.

Zedoc noticed their condition and decided that they were just not eating as they should. So, he decided to make them eat the food he brought them. He started with Boren and forced his mouth open and started pushing the food down his throat.

Boren started choking on the food. He couldn't breathe and was turning blue. Zedoc got scared and stopped. He didn't want his new friends to die. They were all he had now, except for his rats. He loved his rats, but these boys were so much more fun to have around. He could boss them and make them do things for him. So he shook Boren and tried to get him to start breathing again.

Boren vomited and finally started to breathe. Zedoc slapped him for vomiting up his food. He considered the food something he fixed special for them. He did use his rat's crap after all. He considered it to be very nutritious. He didn't eat it himself, of course. He reserved it for his new friends.

Kedron was screaming at Zedoc to stop. He couldn't bear to have his friend suffer like that. He couldn't believe Zedoc would force him to eat that terrible food. It wasn't food, it was garbage that needed to be thrown out.

Zedoc let Boren go and headed for Kedron. "Ah guess ya'll ud do better? Wanna let me try to feed ya? Ah'm sure Ah cud get some of it down ya. Come on, man! Ya gotta eat!"

"I'm not eating that shit! I've tried, but it makes me vomit. If you can't feed us real food, we will die for sure. Look at us! We're starving!"

Zedoc didn't like the way his new friend was talking to him, but Kedron was making some kind of sense. Maybe the food he was trying to get them to eat really was terrible. He decided to taste it just to be sure.

"Since ya'll know so much, Ah'll try it m'self." As soon as Zedoc put some in his mouth, he vomited it back out. He realized then that it wasn't any good at all. In fact, it really was terrible.

After wiping his mouth on his sleeve, he said, "Well now, Ah guess yer right. This stuff is shit! Ef Ah caint eat it, ya'll shouldn't either. From now on, Ah'll feed ya whut Ah eat. Maybe then ya'll will fatten up a bit.

Ah honestly don' want ya ta die. Ah want ya fer mah friends to hep me 'roun here."

"So now Ah'm gon change things just a bit. Ya'll keep yer beds the same to protect you from the rats and to keep ya'll here with me. Got that? But Ah'll change yer food to wut Ah eat. Yer werk is gettin' better, but the place still stinks. So w'll jus'keep the werk drill the same."

Kedron spoke up again, "You know, Zedoc, if the water was clean, maybe the place would get clean too. We're just smearing the stink around and not getting it off anything. If you really want us to do a better job, we need clean water."

Zedoc was becoming angry with Kedron now. "Well, mister smarty pants, Ah'll give it some thought, but don' be tellin'me what ta do. Ah hates it."

"Okay, you're the boss, Zedoc." Kedron didn't want to make Zedoc any more upset. He knew it could go very bad for him if he did.

The next morning, Zedoc brought them the food he liked to eat. It was better than the rat shit, but not by a lot. At least they could keep it down. They half-feared that the meat in the stew was rat. But they really didn't want to know. So they ate in silence.

Zedoc apparently decided to try following Kedron's advice about the clean water. Because that same day, he brought in buckets of it for the boys to use on the floor and walls. The boys worked hard that day and the smell did get better.

Zedoc noticed the difference and said so.

The next thing the boys wanted to work on with Zedoc was getting the rats out of the house or at least confined to one area of the house.

A few weeks later, Boren suggested to Zedoc that maybe if the rats could stay out of the kitchen, it might be easier to keep clean. Zedoc flew into a rage at such a suggestion.

"Mah rats is mah family. It wud hurt them to be kept out of the kitchen or anywhere else. Ah caint buleev ya'll ud say somthin' like that."

Boren was frightened by Zedoc's anger. He didn't know what to say, so he kept his mouth shut. Maybe Zedoc would think about it and change his mind later. He could only hope.

The boys had come to realize that the cages they slept in really did keep them safe from the rats. Sometimes they would come close to the door and watch them, their red eyes bright in the dark. It was terrifying. They both knew that those rats would eat them if given the chance.

They were also grateful that their food was a bit better. At least now they had started to gain a little weight. They had been on the verge of starvation. They were lucky Zedoc had noticed when he did. They would not have lasted much longer on their previous diet. Now, they needed to plan a way of escape.

CHAPTER 12

RESCUING JARRONE

LATER IN THE day, Magg went to Donavan to talk to him about the feeling she was having that there was someone close by who had really strong magic.

"Donavan, have you felt the pull of someone with real magic not far from here?"

"Now that you mention it, I have felt echoes of magic that I could not explain. It must be someone with really powerful magic for us to feel it. What are you thinking? Should one of us try to find him or her and bring them here?"

"That's exactly what I'm thinking. The problem is that the evil one is closing in and might get there before we do."

"Then we'd better decide and get on it right away. I don't want this person to fall victim to the evil one on their own."

"I think I should go. I have the stronger magic and might better be able to defend this person. What are your feelings, Donavan?"

"I would almost rather go myself, but you do have a point. With Zarcon here, I think we could defend the others pretty well. So, if you go, go swiftly. Who will you take with you? You cannot go alone."

Magg smiled at his concern, "Well, since you insist, I would take Matton and the new soldier, Tenzi, with me. The three of us should be fine on the trail and getting this person back here quickly."

"Just one thing, Magg. Have Matton bring that horn of his to warn us when you're near to Anakik. That way we'll be ready for you and the battle. I'm sure you'll be coming in pretty fast at that point."

"That's a great idea, Donavan. I'll make sure Matton has it with him when we leave."

"Alright, but get moving, you know there isn't much time until the evil one gets here or there."

Magg headed for Matton and Tenzi who were taking care of the horses at the time. She was glad they were there so they could get started right away.

"Matton, Tenzi, we have a mission to go find a person with magic. They aren't far from here, but we need to get there before they are destroyed by the evil one. And Matton, would you please bring your horn so we can warn Donavan and the others that we're coming back in with the one who has magic?"

Matton agreed and found his horn. They started saddling the horses for their ride. Within just a few moments, they were on their way out of the village to the rescue.

Magg led the way. She could sense where the magic was coming from and in which direction to travel to get there quickly. Matton was close behind with Tenzi taking up the rear.

Magg and her two friends were making really good time in their rescue mission to find the person with magic. The journey was a bit rough with the track ahead being narrow and rocky. They didn't dare try the main road for fear of the evil one finding them. They were swift yet careful. They could not afford to have any of the horses get injured on the way.

The forest was thick with many trees just off the trail. There seemed to be many forest animals moving through the brush as though they were trying to escape something headed their way. The uneasiness of the group grew as more and more animals rushed pass them. They knew then that evil was truly close by.

Magg turned to the others, "I'm really nervous about this mission. There seems to be something going on among the animals here that is frightening them. I hope we're not going to be too late to rescue whoever it is. I feel the magic as being very strong and powerful. I really want to meet this person and help them get away."

Matton spoke up, "We'll make it I'm sure. I know we can't be very far away. I even feel some power getting closer. I just hope it's from our person of magic and not the evil thing coming closer too."

"Oh, Matton, I hope you're right. We really need anyone with magic now to help us. Time is growing short for all of us, I fear. I'm hoping the person we seek will have powerful magic. I sense this evil is a form of ancient magic. I know we will need all the help we can get to fight it."

Just then, Magg looked ahead through the trees and could see the village. "Look! There's the village just ahead! Hurry, we're almost there!"

So, the three of them urged their horses forward and came into the village hoping to find the person with magic quickly. The village was quiet and it seemed that the homes were boarded up or locked down against some danger. Magg knew it was probably because the person with magic had warned them of what was coming. It was now even more critical that they find that person.

So they rode to the other edge of town and found Jarrone in a field near a two-story house with what looked like his sister. It appeared to them that he was practicing some spell. Jarrone had found the spell in his mother's Book of Magic. It was one that he had been practicing just this morning.

Magg could see that it was one that a person with magic could alter the perception of anyone or anything nearby. Just now he was making a small mouse look as big as a large dog. His sister jumped back with fear in her eyes until she realized it wasn't real. They both laughed until they saw Magg and the two men approaching them.

Jarrone moved Revinia behind him saying, "Who are you and what do you want here?" He did notice the true character of Magg. He was sure she meant no harm, only to help.

Magg answered, "My name is Magg and these two men are my friends, Matton and Tenzi. They came with me to help. What is your name? We are so glad to have found you."

"My name is Jarrone and this is my sister, Revinia. Tell me what this is all about."

"We have felt magic here and want to rescue you from the evil that is coming. Have you felt it? Will you come with us and join us in our fight against it? We have been preparing for the battle that is surely coming and can use all the help you can offer. I can see that you are powerful. The spell you just performed is a difficult one for one so young and just starting out with the magic. We really do need you."

"Yes, I felt it. I know it is coming and almost here. I have warned my neighbors and told them to lock down their homes until the evil passes. I can only hope it's enough to protect them.

"But come with you where? I have my family here that I must care for. I can't leave them in danger whatever you say. They need me and I need them."

"It's not far from here, but we must hurry. You must know that if you stay here, you will all be destroyed! How many are there in your family? Do you have enough horses for them to come with us now? Time is very short."

"There are five of us. Yes, we have horses, but my father is very frail. He wouldn't last long on a horse. I don't know what to say."

Just then his father came out of the house with his daughter, Lucintha, and his son, Hoskins. He sounded indignant, "What's this about me being so frail that I would not be able to ride a horse? Jarrone, you know I have been on a horse most of my life. I will come with you and survive to tell the tale. You just wait and see! And just where do you think we're going in such a hurry anyway?"

Jarrone wanted to argue, but he could see the determination in his father's eyes. So he said, "Alright, father, let's get the horses saddled and get out of here. This woman, Magg, claims she can rescue us and take us to safety not far from here. I feel the evil coming, as I've told you. So, hurry and let's be off!"

His father said, "Well then, if that's what we need to do, let's be at it! You know the horse I like."

The three siblings along with Magg, Matton, and Tenzi hurried to the stable to saddle the horses while his father waited nearby. When they got to the stable, they could see that the horses looked well and strong.

Magg finally had hope that they would succeed in getting them all out of there before it was too late.

The horses were saddled quickly with everyone helping. Soon, they were all on horses and headed out of the village. Jarrone did have to help his father just a bit to get up on his horse. But that was all that was needed. Magg was hopeful that they had found Jarrone and his family in time to save them all. She knew the evil was closing in on them.

Magg lead the way back to Anakik with Jarrone and his family close behind. Matton and Tenzi brought up the rear in case of trouble. They moved swiftly through the forest joining the animals that were fleeing from what was coming. They had to watch out for them as they were running in a panic and not really watching the horses. Even the larger animals were mostly interested in getting away.

Jarrone's father was keeping up with the group and seemed to be enjoying himself. Jarrone was almost laughing to see him this way. He had been acting invalid for months.

Revinia and Lucintha were becoming a bit aggravated at their father to see him like this. They are the ones who had cared for him for so long. It was obvious that he enjoyed the attention. Things would definitely change when they got settled in their new village. Jarrone could only smile.

The road was rough and narrow-going, but they were all good riders and their horses were strong. There was a little sun coming through the trees, enough so that they could see the trail ahead. Revinia and Lucintha were having a little trouble staying on their horses because of the dresses they were wearing. They had to hang on and just keep going, their lives depended on it. They could feel the danger coming swiftly toward them. They had escaped just in time.

CHAPTER 13

THE BATTLE IS COMING

NEBERON SUDDENLY FELT the magic he was seeking moving swiftly away from him. He would not spend time on the villagers here. He wanted to destroy those with magic and then come back and destroy the villagers later.

He felt the one with the very powerful magic moving away as well. He was furious. Now, he would be facing not only the young man with the wild magic, but the one he tried hard not to fear. That person would be very dangerous to him indeed.

He was not sure he could destroy both of them. Then there was the knowledge that there were others with magic that he might have to eliminate first. This was becoming a very big problem. He only hoped he was more powerful than them all. But he could not know this until the battle was joined.

He knew then that he must move forward with some caution. He would move carefully and watchfully as he made his way to the village where they would be staying. He wanted to be the one that surprised them, not the other way around. He hated surprises. He urged Negra forward at a slow pace taking in the sounds and smells around him. He would lose the element of surprise by doing anything suspicious now. He did not realize that they already knew he was coming and were preparing for him.

He stayed close to the forest edge in order to blend in with his surroundings. His essence of evil would go before him. He could not help that. But those he sought would not know when he would strike. He was counting on the element of surprise to give him the upper hand in the battle to come.

The ground was soft and made moving quietly possible. The track was just a bit damp and muffled any sound Negra might make.

～

Magg and Jarrone could both sense the evil growing closer as they frantically road away. Magg rode ahead with Jarrone and his family following after her with Matton and Tenzi bringing up the rear.

After they had been riding for a while, Jarrone's father was beginning to tire, but he refused to give in to it. He rode with his head held high and his back straight. There was even a small smile on his face.

Jarrone was so proud of his father at this moment. Jarrone knew that at the end of this frantic ride, his father would likely collapse but he would survive. He was tough for his age, more so than any of his children guessed. He had acted dependent on them for some time now and they never bothered to test his strength in all that time. He seemed so content to let others help him and let him rest. Now, he was showing them what he truly was made of and they were proud of him; a little irritated, but proud.

The forest flew by as they rushed to safety in Anakik. Time was not on their side at this moment. Neberon was closing in on them. He had figured out where they were and was hot on their trail. Luckily, their goal was not far ahead. They just needed another mile and they would be there. Magg felt the evil thing getting closer, but not in a hurry now. It seemed to be taking its time following them. This made Magg more nervous, but grateful to have a slight reprieve.

Matton had his horn ready to alert the village that they were coming in fast. He blew it now.

Zarcon and Donavan heard the horn and made ready for battle. They knew that Matton would only blow that horn if they were in danger. The villagers knew what to do as well. They gathered their families together and moved into the forest where they could hide so the battle would not affect them as much, they hoped. The villagers found places to stay until it was deemed safe to come back into the village. If the battle went the wrong way, they would stay in the forest and head for the next village to the north.

The children knew what it meant for them to go into the forest as they had not done it before. Even with the mist monsters, they had stayed at home. This was new and somewhat frightening to them. Some of the younger children started to cry. Their parents comforted them and reminded them that crying was going to draw the attention of the evil thing that was coming. This scared them into complete silence. None of them even dared cough.

Donavan and Zarcon were grateful that the villagers remembered their instructions and left their homes. It would not do for those fighting the evil to have to worry about the safety of the villagers on top of trying to eliminate the evil thing. Magic could be dangerous and uncontrolled at times in battle. No one wanted to cause the villagers injury with their magic.

Just then, Magg and the rest poured into Anakik. Donavan and Zarcon were surprised to see so many with her. Magg yelled for Donavan to help Jarrone's father off his horse. It was plain to see that he was about to fall off. Matton helped get him into the inn nearby so he could rest.

Jarrone and his siblings were off their horses quickly along with Magg and Matton. Tenzi had already been gathering up the horses' reins to guide them to the stable on the edge of the village. He was concerned for their safety as well. He was brushing them down and getting them fed when Jasmine came in to see how things were going.

"Tenzi, you are such a great help to us. Taking care of the horses is so very important and the rest of us seem to have forgotten that. Please know that we really appreciate your concern for them."

"Thank you, Jasmine, it has been important to me to do the things that others sometimes forget. The horses saved us from what could have been certain death. I'm not sure about that, but it seemed so to me at the time. They were valiant in getting us here safely. I wanted them to know that I cared and appreciated them by doing what needed to be done for them."

"Can you join us now? Are the horses quite taken care of for now? You are needed to help us understand what happened and why this young man's family needed to be here with us."

"I will be glad to come and contribute what I can to the story. I worry that too much talk might allow the evil that approaches to attack while we're busy doing nothing to prepare. But I will come now."

Jasmine seemed to wake up at that. She had been under the illusion that they would have time to plan and discuss what was going on since Magg left in such a hurry to rescue the others. She told Tenzi to come with her and that they were meeting in the great hall of the inn. They both ran for the inn knowing that time was short.

The others were gathered there discussing what must be done before the evil arrived. It was even at the door. Fortunately, they had discussed the situation previously and so they only had to find out what Jarrone could do to help. He was telling them of his most powerful spells that he had learned from his mother and from her Book of Spells.

Zarcon was especially impressed. Jarrone knew things that had taken him years to master. This young man was so much more powerful than he even realized. Between him and Magg, with Donavan and himself, he was certain they had the advantage over whatever was coming.

Zarcon had been studying his Book of Spells and Magic about what was most likely coming. In it, he had found the history of the order of wizards anciently. He learned that this being was ancient and that his name was likely Neberon. He was a rebel in his early life and did things not allowed then. He had been dismissed from his home with the other wizards. Now, he was on the loose again. It was also likely that he had been the creator of the mist monsters and maybe even the Black Wind. The fact that this group of friends had destroyed both would explain why he was after them now.

He decided to explain all that to his friends and to remind them that it would be one against the four of them. Surely, there would be a way to stop it, maybe even forever.

Everyone was in shock at this news, but it made sense. Zarcon had given them the reason and possible motive of this thing coming to destroy them and anyone else with magic.

Magg spoke up, "All this makes sense, Zarcon. Now we know what we're up against. I know that Jarrone is going to be of great value to us in the coming battle. I have also found deeper wells of magic that I can teach you all. But it might have to wait for a quieter time when this is over with. I feel the evil one is very close and coming in very angry. So we'd better be ready and not allow it the opportunity to surprise us unaware. We mostly need to protect everyone no matter from which direction it comes at us."

Zarcon was again amazed at the power that emanated from Magg. Jarrone was very close behind. Donavan was learning quickly as well. Maybe he didn't need to worry about who would take over after he was gone. Now, there were three with such powerful magic that he was truly in awe of them.

It was agreed where each of those with magic would stand guard. Whoever engaged the evil thing first would call out to the others. They would not be far apart so that they could get to each other swiftly. Each entrance to the village would be covered. They knew it was just a matter of moments until they were attacked.

CHAPTER 14

ESCAPE

I**T HAD BEEN** many days since Boren had suggested keeping the rats out of the kitchen. Zedoc was obviously thinking about it. He kept looking at the rats and seeing what they were actually doing to the kitchen that he and the boys were trying to keep clean.

Finally, Zedoc called the boys to him and said, "Well, Ah bin thinkin' a lot about wut ya'll said about the rats bein' in the kitchen. Ah kin see that ya'll are rite about them makin' a mess that we bin tryin to clean up ever day. So, how do ya'll think we kin keep em out?"

Boren said, "Kedron and I think maybe we could put up some barricades at the entry to the kitchen and see if that keeps them out. There's some wood in the shed outback we could see from the window there. Maybe we could build something together?"

"Ya know, that's exacly wut Ah wuz thinkin'. Cud we draw up a pichur and build it? Ah'll git the wud frum the shed and cut it fer the whatcha call it?"

"The barricade?"

"Yup, that's it!"

"When do you want to start?"

"How 'bout in the mornin'?"

Boren and Kedron could hardly contain their excitement. They said at once, "Perfect!"

The day was ending, Zedoc fed them and sent them to their cages for the night. They were getting used to the routine now.

When Zedoc had gone to bed, they started planning their escape. It had been a long time coming, but they knew what they needed to do now.

"Alright," said Kedron, "Let's figure this out. We'll be inside waiting for Zedoc to bring in the wood, right? While he's busy gathering the wood, we head for the back door. I'm hoping the rats won't give us away. They're pretty smart. You know how to ride a horse, don't you, Boren?"

"I do indeed. We did see a horse in Zedoc's barn, didn't we? I can ride bare back if necessary, can you?"

"I can if I have you to hold on to."

"This will be our one chance to get out of this stinking place. We can't fail."

"I know. I hope that horse is still there. What if it isn't? Do we just run for it?"

"We might have to, I hope not."

"Remember, we haven't even been walking for weeks. So, let's pray for the horse to get us out of here."

They finally fell asleep with high hopes.

~

Morning came and Zedoc came down the stairs to let them know he was ready to start working.

"Get up, ya lazy boys! We got werk ta do."

Boren said, "We're ready to work! It will be so good for all of us to work together to build the barricades. I sure hope we have plenty of wood!"

"Well, Ah chekt on it las' nite and it looks to be plenty fer wut we're doin'."

"That's good to hear! Let's get busy then, alright?"

So, they all went up the stairs and Zedoc went outside to start gathering the wood for their project.

Boren said, "NOW!"

They ran out the back door and headed for the barn. It was such a relief to see the horse there. Boren grabbed the bridle and got it on the horse. They used a bale of hay close by to get up on the horse. Boren lifted Kedron up behind him and they were ready to flee.

As they were headed for the barn door, they could see Zedoc coming at a fast pace. He knew what they were planning and was going to try to stop them.

Boren kicked the horse and he started to run. They brushed past Zedoc and knocked him down.

"Ya'll are horse thieves!! Bring 'im back! Ah'll git you fur this. Ah thought we wuz frenz!" There was actual pain in his voice as they hurried to the road to get away.

The horse wasn't much, but he was faster than if they had to run. They couldn't have made it without him. It didn't take long before the horse had to slow down and rest. But they were far enough away to be sure Zedoc couldn't catch them.

They stopped to let the horse rest and eat some grass. They were both so amazed and excited to be free at last! They hugged each other and started to cry. It had been so hard.

They didn't know if they were even headed in the right direction. They only knew they wanted to find Zarcon and his friends. They didn't care how far they had to go. They would find a way to keep going until they found him.

CHAPTER 15

THE BATTLE

NEBERON IS APPROACHING the area near the village of Anakik to begin his vengeance on any who were there that had magic and had been killing off his precious mist monsters. Included in his desire for vengeance was Zarcon, Donavan, Magg, and now Jarrone that Neberon was unsure of. He would also attack the villagers if he had the chance.

Now, he must decide from which entry he would attack. He could sense magic all around the village as if they knew he was coming and had prepared. Since he had been counting on the element of surprise, he became concerned as to how he would do that. He thought maybe if he waited a few hours or even days, they would become complacent and decide that maybe he wouldn't attack after all. Putting it off did not appeal to him in the least. But he must do something to change what was happening now.

He realized that if they were prepared to fight him, that maybe they would be able to eliminate him before he could do any damage to them. Neberon had a really big problem now. He didn't really know what to do.

Negra began to paw the ground in impatience. He acted as though he wanted to get to it and join the battle that he had been hoping for for a very long time. He could sense Neberon's hesitation. Negra did not understand it. He was very intelligent for a horse and had known Neberon for millennia but this was a new thing.

Neberon had stayed in his cave for millennia but when on occasion he left the cave, it was to swiftly eliminate anything that had disturbed his rest. Now, he was slow and cautious. It had never happened before. Negra was confused and becoming angry. His eyes were glowing red now. He continued pawing the earth beneath him. He was on the verge of rebellion. Neberon finally realized that Negra was about to rebel against him if he didn't figure out what he was going to do next. The problem was, he still couldn't decide. So much depended on his success that he began to doubt whether he could succeed against the magic he would face.

This was the reason he left his cave after all. He had to do whatever he could to destroy those who had killed off his mist monsters and ruined his Black Wind. Remembering all that they had done to his creations helped him build the rage he needed to continue with his goal of destruction. He had to remember how great it would feel when it was over and he could go back and cause the villagers he had let live to die a slow and painful death.

He finally felt ready to do what he came here for, so he urged Negra forward. Negra nearly leapt to it. It was such a relief to be moving forward and getting on with why they came here. Neberon moved forward and decided to go into Anakik by the main road. He knew those with magic were aware that he was coming, so why try to surprise anyone? It felt ridiculous now.

As he approached the entrance to the village, he could hear one of the wizards yelling to the others to come. Neberon was a bit irritated by it, but tried not to let it bother him too much. He had work to do here after all.

~

Donavan was the one to see Neberon coming his way. He yelled to Magg and the others that he was coming. The others rushed to help Donavan. Jarrone was there figuring out which of his spells he would like to use first. He was young yet.

Neberon decided to enter on Negra to make a chilling entrance. He knew that Negra was frightening and would add to his image of evil power. As he came closer, he knew he had to do something violent to set the stage for his battle.

He had decided to start with a serious, nasty spell. He was hoping to take out at least two of his opponents at once. He began by chanting a complicated spell. He started forming a ball of flame between his hands. He was aiming for the two men in the center of the group. He was ready to throw it at them. It was to be a magnificent show of power.

Magg could see what he was doing and started a spell of her own. She was using one that would counteract Neberon's. She chose to form ice between her hands and direct it toward Neberon just as he was throwing his spell at Donavan and Jarrone. Her spell hit the flame just as it was thrown. It quickly stopped the flame and put it out. It fizzled in a very sad display of what Neberon thought would be fabulous.

Neberon was in rage that his spell could be destroyed so easily. He realized it was done by the one he feared most. This woman was extremely powerful. He started to worry as he had not before. But he must finish his work here or lose his reputation as the most powerful wizard in the world. Could he succeed? He must. So he decided on another spell that would make an impression on any looking on. He watched where the powerful one was as he got started on his spell. This one had to work.

Neberon chose one of his most powerful spells next. He began the spell but did it quickly so that it would be more difficult to mount a counter attack. He used the spell he had chosen for the first village. It was the one that brought glass flying in all directions. He chanted a few words of magic and sent it at Donavan.

As it hit the ground in front of Donavan and Magg, it exploded into shards of red glass. Donavan barely had time to create a shield around them all before they could be injured. However, one shard hit Zarcon. He was standing just out of the circle of the shield created by Donavan. Donavan had been unaware of his whereabouts as he formed the shield.

Magg ran to him immediately to care for his injury. His shoulder had been hit and caused enough damage that Magg had to take him to the inn to heal him. Zarcon had been keeping to the side in order to help as needed. Now, he was injured and couldn't help at all. After Magg healed him, she told him he must rest for a while. Jasmine had stayed at the inn in case she was needed. Now, she was grateful she could take care of Zarcon. She helped get him settled in his room in the inn. Then she stayed with him to keep him company.

Zarcon was not happy about having to be away from the battle. He did, however, realize it was probably for the best since he was hurt. He was also very glad that Jasmine was there too. She helped calm him and settle his emotions as much as she could. Greta was still recovering and stayed with one of the families in the forest until the battle ended or they could finally go back to the village.

Magg was quick to return to the battle. She knew Jasmine would be there for Zarcon. While she was away, Jarrone had sent one of his spells toward Neberon that caused him to be frozen. Neberon was shocked that he couldn't move. This young man was using really strong magic against him. He was able to free himself after a moment or two, but it had brought doubt into his mind that he was invincible. Neberon was too powerful for it to last longer. In fact, Neberon smiled and said, "So, you think you can defeat me so easily? It will take much more than that to cause me harm. What else can you do, young wizard?" He said the last with as much scorn as he could put into it.

Jarrone was embarrassed, but quickly came up with a stronger one and sent it into Neberon immediately. He was able to catch Neberon on fire and let him burn. Again, Neberon was shocked at the spell. It did indeed burn him and he knew that if he didn't get it stopped, that he could possibly die. This could not be either! Neberon had to draw on his own spell to cool the fire and escape being burned alive. He tried to play it down and acted as if it was nothing. "So, you have learned new tricks? Very good! But you still must do better than that."

Jarrone was beginning to doubt his ability. He had no idea of the real effect he was having on Neberon. In fact, he was unaware of his power even then. He was embarrassed again and almost went to the inn to hide, but didn't, he knew he really might be needed.

As Magg came near, Neberon got nervous. He knew she was powerful, maybe even more powerful than he was. He must eliminate her before she could do him harm. Jarrone had really shaken him up, but he couldn't show it.

He started another spell that sent wheels of fire toward Magg's head. He hoped to cut it off. He let it loose and steered Negra behind the village wall to watch what happened.

But Magg saw it coming in time to counter it with a blocking spell that sent it right back to Neberon. She saw where he had tried to hide. He ducked just in time to avoid losing his own head. He was becoming a bit frightened now. Things were definitely not going his way. He was grateful to have Negra with him. He was more courageous with his horse under him. Negra was fearless.

Magg was tired of countering his magic so she decided to go on the attack. She wanted to do Neberon real harm this time. She decided to use a spell she had seen her sister Zora use on others. It made her nervous, but Neberon was evil and must be stopped. So, she sent a spell to freeze Neberon and then called for biting flies to come to him. She made his mouth stay open so the flies could get inside him. He couldn't move, only struggle against the pain of the flies eating him from the inside. He fell off Negra and hit the ground.

Neberon was in great agony and he couldn't stop the spell. His eyes turned vivid blood red and shown like red coals. It was horrifying. His rage knew no bounds at the humiliation of being knocked off Negra and being unable to stop Magg's spell. That had never happened to him before. He had always been the most powerful wizard ever. Now he was being treated like a common magician. He could not bear it.

Finally, Neberon remembered a spell he had used anciently that had stopped this kind of spell. He used his hands to conjure the spell and it melted the flies inside him and healed his organs before they were gone completely. He vomited the fly remains while he was on the ground. He was feeling sick, weary, and in pain.

Then Negra became enraged. He started pawing the ground as if he would attack Magg for humiliating his master. His eyes also began to glow dark blood red. He reared and charged. No one knew for sure what he intended to do so Jarrone, Donavan, and Magg sent powerful spells at him before he could get very far. They meant to stop him only, but all the power that was sent into him caused him to burn into a pile of greasy ashes on the spot.

Neberon screamed in pain. Negra was almost his friend, the only living thing that had been with him for the eons of his life. He was shocked and dismayed to see his precious Negra destroyed so easily. He was at a loss as to what to do. He feared his fate would be the same if he didn't do something desperate.

He dug deep into his magic and brought out his most powerful spell. It was supposed to end the battle once and for all. He knew if he used it and it wasn't successful, he would be finished. He was weakening from the use of the magic so far and this was his last effort. He was so angry that he just did not care anymore.

He directed this spell at all those with magic. It was like his Black Wind, but not as big. He formed it and a spiraling cloud began to form. It grew bigger as the others watched. Neberon sent it to them. Just as he was thinking this would surely work and end the battle quickly.

It turned out to be too big for one person to stop or counter attack. Magg looked at Donavan and Jarrone, and together they were just able to send it back to Neberon. It took all three to generate enough power to do so. Neberon's wind was very impressive. But together they had been able to redirect it back to him.

The last they saw of Neberon was the look of horror on his face as the wind hit him and sent him backward. Magg dug deep into her magic and found a way to create a portal that would take him to another world. As Neberon disappeared, they could hear him screaming in rage and anger.

Suddenly, it was over and so quiet. Jasmine had been watching from the inn and came running as soon as it was over. She hurled herself into Donavan's arms as fast as she could get to him. He held her close and kissed her face. He was so grateful to be alive and have Jasmine there to love him.

Matton had also been hiding near the inn to worry about Magg and make sure she survived. When it was over, he, too, ran to Magg and held her. Magg almost collapsed in his arms. She was so exhausted from the magic she had used to create the portal for Neberon that she could hardly stand. She was grateful for Matton's concern.

No one spoke for a bit, it was so hard to believe they had all survived. They noticed Jarrone standing alone and called him over for a group hug. He had been an important part of the battle whether he believed it or not.

Finally, everyone started talking at once.

"Is he really gone? Magg! What have you done? Wait 'til Zarcon hears about this!"

After a few moments of talking with the others, Jarrone left to go find his family. He needed comfort too. It had been far more frightening than he had ever thought it could be. The others bid him goodbye as he walked away.

Donavan looked at Magg with new eyes, as did Matton. They both acted as if they might be just a bit frightened of her. She had magic that was unheard of. How had she created the portal? It was so amazing. They really were afraid of the power it must have taken to create it. They were a bit concerned that Magg had called the biting flies on Neberon, but they would talk about that later. It seemed against everything they thought Magg was all about. It was so cruel and Magg had sworn not to be cruel. Neberon was indeed evil and maybe that's how she justified the use of the flies. Donavan knew they must talk about it.

Just then, Magg started to go down. Matton was close and caught her before she fell. It was plain that the magic she had used came with a price. Matton carried Magg to the inn where she could rest. Seeing her nearly pass out was frightening too.

The innkeeper, Aribon, was there and had been hiding behind his bar when Matton walked in carrying Magg. He came at once and showed Matton to her room on the main floor.

Donavan and Jasmine followed him to make sure Magg would be alright.

Matton laid her down on the bed and sat by her in the chair close by. He held her hand and spoke softly to her.

"Magg, how are you feeling? That was amazing what you did back there. It must have taken all the rest of whatever strength it took to do it. But don't do it again any time soon, alright?"

Magg could barely talk, "Matton, it did take all I had to create that portal for Neberon. I've never done anything like that before and didn't know I could. I had to dig so deep into the magic that I thought for a moment I might die trying. But I had to do it or all would have been lost. I truly hope I never have to do it again. It was so exhausting and kind of terrifying, too."

Donavan and Jasmine walked in just then. Donavan spoke up, "Magg, you continue to amaze me. I hope when you feel better and are rested up, you can teach me a little of that magic. It was very impressive. I think you could be the most powerful wizard, or is it witch, this world has known. Xyrene was powerful, he did create the Blue Orb, but I never heard of him creating a portal to other worlds.

"Now that I think about it. Zarcon and I did send the Blue Orb to another world, but it took both of us to do it. The witches helped us even though they didn't know it at the time. You've done it alone. Amazing!"

Magg was obviously growing increasingly sleepy. "Now, I need to sleep it off. Would you all mind leaving me to it? Matton, please stay with me. I don't want to be alone right now."

"Of course, I want to be near you while you sleep."

After the others left, Matton got up on the bed with Magg and held her as she slept.

Meanwhile, Jarrone found his family and spent the rest of the day and night with them. They were able to comfort him. It was obvious that he had been through a lot and needed to rest and recover.

His father said, "I'm so very proud of you and your magic. Your mother would be proud of you too. She loved you dearly."

"Thanks father, I really needed that vote of confidence. I'm not sure whether I made a difference or not. But I gave it my best. Neberon was really strong and I felt not so strong trying to fight him with magic."

"I'm thinking you made more difference than you can know."

Jarrone was so grateful that he had been there to help the others. Neberon was one scary creature. At least now he was gone from this world.

As Donavan and Jasmine left Magg and Matton alone, they decided they had better tell Zarcon all about what had happened while he was resting. Zarcon was feeling better, but he didn't seem to be healing as he should.

"Zarcon, you wouldn't believe what Magg did today. That Neberon creature had thrown a spell at us that was beyond anything the rest of us were prepared for. Magg looked at Jarrone and I and we used all our magic to counteract his spell. Our spell knocked him away, but then Magg opened a portal to send him to another world. It was kind of like when we sent the Blue Orb away, remember?"

Zarcon was excited to hear about Magg and all she could do. "Yes, I remember, that was something, wasn't it? Now, you tell me that Magg did it on her own? She is almost frighteningly powerful. I'm so glad she has a good heart and Matton to love her."

"I agree, Zarcon. When it was over, I really was so much in awe that it was very close to fear. Maybe we should talk about what we can do about all that. But later, we all need rest after this terrible day."

"That sounds like a good idea to me, Donavan. Let's all rest for now and discuss things in the morning."

Jasmine and Donavan left Zarcon to rest while they went to their own room to do the same.

CHAPTER 16

A CELEBRATION PLANNED

THE MORNING DAWNED bright and clear. The sky was a glorious blue as if to celebrate the end of Neberon. The villagers came back to their homes and settled back in with their families. There was much talk of a celebration with the entire village. It would be the best and biggest one yet. There was an air of joy that had not existed until now.

Plans were being made and decorations started appearing. Aribon, the innkeeper volunteered to prepare the meat and vegetables if the villagers would bring the rest. Everyone was more than happy to supply what was needed to make a truly wonderful feast. Some made fabulous desserts, others made wonderful drinks to mix and share. A few even had some homemade ale to add to the festivities. It was going to be grand.

Donavan and Jasmine were a bit late getting out of their room that morning. It had been a long loving night for both of them. It was indeed great to be alive and celebrate it together. It seems fear can bring much stronger feelings of love when the fear passes.

Magg was still trying to recover from the use of so much magic that she felt the need to rest awhile longer. Matton was eager to spend the day with her and make sure she would be well soon.

Zarcon seemed to be a bit worn out and his wound was bothering him. Greta was finally able to come see him and take care of his wound. She could see that it might not be healing as it should. She changed the dressings and put some salve on it that was supposed to help it heal. But whatever it was was beyond her ability. She knew she would need Magg to come soon.

Greta herself felt great, especially now that the evil one was no longer in this world. She had been so excited to hear what had happened during the battle. She was amazed once again at what Magg could do. The new wizard, Jarrone, was also someone she wanted to meet and find out what kind of young man he was with so much magic at such a young age. Life was becoming more interesting all the time. Her only concern was for Zarcon.

Jarrone was glad there would be a celebration to take all their minds off the horrors of the past few weeks. He was going to enjoy spending time with his family and meet new friends in the village. Revinia and Lucintha were also interested in the celebration and making new friends. Hoskins was in his own world looking at the animals nearby in the forest. He did love the animals.

Jarrone's father had needed a lot of rest after his wild ride. He was happy he could prove to his children that he wasn't the invalid they seemed to think he was. The downside was that now they knew he wasn't the invalid they thought he was. He was going to have to do more for himself so the children could have a life of their own now. Oh well, life was more interesting now. He was discovering that he had a bit more self-respect doing for himself as he should.

In the meantime, the villagers were setting up tables and benches for the celebration. They were hoping for maybe a bit of a magic show from their friends with magic. The children were especially hoping for fireworks or something as exciting. Today was a day for fun and food.

There were several members of the village who had musical instruments and were practicing for the dance that was to be held later that evening. The women were cooking and getting ready for the celebration and what to wear. The men were building more tables and benches for the celebration. There was much to prepare and the villagers were enjoying every minute of it. Their lives had just changed into one of joy and safety like they had not had for many years.

Now that the mist monsters were gone; the Black Wind was destroyed; and their creator, Neberon was gone forever; they knew that only time would tell if this life of joy would continue. For now, no thought was given to the future and possible difficulties, it was time for feeling safe and happy in the moment.

CHAPTER 17

THE BOYS FIND SOLVIG

B OREN AND KEDRON were getting close to a village. It was getting late and they needed to stop for the night. They were hoping for some help. It turned out to be Solvig, Jarrone's village. As they entered the village, it was plain to see that there was an air of joy among the villagers. They had just gotten word from Anakik that Neberon had been destroyed. They were finally safe from that evil creature. It was said that his horse had also been destroyed. Such good news!

When one of the villagers, Karmine, a tall broad-shouldered man with a black beard and shoulder-length hair, spotted the two small boys coming into the village on a raggedy horse, he knew something was amiss. He called his wife to come and see them. He could tell they needed help.

"My, what brings two small boys into our village riding a sorry excuse for a horse?"

"My name is Boren and this is my friend, Kedron. We escaped Neberon by hiding in our cave after everyone else was dead. It was terrible. Then we were held captive by an evil farmer named Zedoc on the other side of the river. We stole his horse to get away."

The two of them were amazed at these two boys and what they had done. It was obvious that there was much more to the story, but it could wait. Right now, it was plain to see that the boys were half-starved and weary from all they had been through.

Karmine's wife, Roslin, was motherly-looking and had beautiful long red hair that she wore in a braid. She said, "It looks like you two could use some food and some rest. Want to come with me and I'll feed you and you can sleep in one of our extra beds for the night. I'm Roslin and that's my husband, Karmine. We have a couple of boys, a little younger than you two. But I'm sure you'll get along just fine."

Gradually, some of the other villagers saw what was going on and came over to find out more about these two strange boys who just rode into their village. One of the women asked, "So, Roslin, are you going to take care of them for the night?"

"I am indeed. They are half-starved and in need of a bath and a long sleep. Do you have a tub and some warmish water, Ruby?"

"I do, bring them over and we'll take care of the cleanup. Stefan, please help me with the tub, would you?" He came to her in a hurry, he knew the boys really needed a bath. They were so very dirty and smelly.

Some of the villagers smiled at that. It was good to see that the boys would be taken care of at least for the night.

The boys were unaware how bad they smelled after spending all that time with Zedoc and his rats. But since it was mentioned, they knew it had to be pretty bad.

Karmine helped them down from the horse telling them he would take care of the "poor thing".

Roslin led them to her house and introduced them to her sons, Mika and Lorin. They were a year or two younger and they liked each other right away. Roslin ordered them to take off their clothes so she could burn them. There was no hope of getting them clean. Then she gave them each one of her husband's shirts to cover them until they got their "cleanup".

Ruby came and got them and they took turns getting clean. Ruby almost cried to see their condition. It was so very sad.

After they were cleaned up, they were taken back to Roslin for clean shirts and underwear. They were so thin that they could wear the clothes of her sons. She had been preparing them food while they were getting cleaned up. As soon as they were settled at the table, she brought them fresh stew and crusty bread. There was plenty of fresh water from their well. After they had eaten, they were almost asleep in their bowls. Roslin and Karmine carried them to the extra bed made up for them. They were asleep as their head hit the pillow. They finally felt safe, clean, and full.

~

The next morning, the sun woke them up as it shown in their bedroom window. Breakfast was ready and Roslin called them and her two sons to come and eat. She and Karmine had already eaten. They wanted to let all the boys sleep in a bit.

Breakfast was bacon, eggs, potatoes, and fresh apple juice that Roslin made and stored in the cellar. Boren and Kedron hadn't eaten this good in months. They ate until they were almost sick. It tasted too good to be real. Roslin's boys were excited to have them as friends. If only they could stay for a while.

After breakfast was eaten and the boys were relaxing together playing games, Roslin called Boren and Kedron to come and talk for a bit.

"I'm so happy we could help you last night. Karmine and I talked it over and decided that you are welcome to stay as long as you would like. I'm thinking you have plans. I would like to know what you are thinking about what I said. What do you need or whom do you seek?"

Kedron spoke up, "It has been so wonderful to stay here with you. We are very grateful. The thing we want most is to find Zarcon and his friends. We are thinking we might have magic and would like to have their help in finding out if we really do."

Roslin smiled, "You're in luck. Zarcon and his friends are in Anakik, not far from here. I'm thinking anyone in the village could help you get there safely. Maybe after you talk to Zarcon, you could stay here for a while. What do you think?"

Boren was confused now. He wanted both things but didn't know quite how it would work. He said, "Maybe if we go meet with Zarcon, we can figure out where we want to stay. I would like it to be here for sure. Would that be alright?"

Roslin smiled, "Of course, whatever you want to do is fine. I'll find someone heading to Anakik and see if you can tag along. What do you think?"

"That would be great! Thanks, Roslin!"

The next day, Boren and Kedron stayed with Roslin and Karmine again. Roslin was checking around the village for anyone going into Anakik for the day. It turned out that one of the men, Andoron, was planning on going in a couple of days.

Roslin let Boren and Kedron know about it. They were both fine with getting to spend more time with Roslin and her family even though they were anxious to get to Zarcon.

What none of them knew was that the young man who was going to take them to Anakik had no intention of doing so. He had other plans for these two boys. He was big and tall. He had a hook nose and moss green, beady eyes. His face was marked by scars no one really knew how he got them. He never spoke of it. He had mousy brown hair that was lank and limp that came just below his shoulders. Why anyone would trust him is beyond comprehension. But he could really put on a good show if he felt the need. He was hoping when he came into Solvig that he would be able to catch at least one child and take them with him when he left the village. He had evil plans and now he could start working on them.

CHAPTER 18

CELEBRATION

T HE CELEBRATION WAS finally about to begin. The food smelled heavenly and everyone was dressed in their best for the event. Of course, Revinia and Lucintha were dressed beautifully and were turning heads of all the young men. The young women were jealous and having a hard time just then. Finally, one of the young girls, Jerona, walked up to them and asked Revinia where her dress came from.

When Revinia told her that she had made it herself, Jerona got really excited, "Revinia, would you make such a dress for us? We could bring you the material if you would. We could pay you, too!"

Revinia was so happy that the other girls wanted to wear the dresses she made. "I would so love to make dresses for all of you under these conditions, of course. I have one promise I need from you. I will make your dress how I want to make it. You cannot tell me how to make it. Is it a deal? I have a certain gift for making these dresses and I must honor my gift."

The girls were all willing to agree, in fact, they were excited to see what Revinia would create for them. They also knew that whatever it was, it would be worth whatever it cost to have one.

And that is how Revinia was able to make a living with her gift of creating beautiful dresses. It was later that the men of the village figured out that the shirts Jarrone and his brother and father were wearing were made by Lucintha and were very well-made. She would become the seamstress for men's shirts in due time. Jarrone's family would be doing very well in Anakik, indeed. But it would take a little time for that to come to full benefit.

Meanwhile, the celebration was getting started with lots of food and getting to know one another. Friendships were made that day that would last lifetimes. They worked together to create a wonderful day for all.

There was roast wild boar, elk, beef, and rabbit. Some of the men had caught fish that were being baked at the inn. Aribon was cooking the meat and loved it. He had a grill and a large oven for the purpose. He also had a fire pit for cooking the meat on a spit. Several of the men were busy turning the spits to cook all that meat.

The smells coming out of the inn were irresistible. He began bringing out platters of meat for the villagers. He also cooked some vegetables such as carrots, peas, squash, potatoes, and beets from the local gardens and his own garden near the inn. There was plenty to eat.

The women brought platters of special desserts and the men brought in the drinks they made year round. There was rum, ale, and beer. One of the families made delicious wine to share. Others brought some fresh spring water that they had near their homes. Others brought apple juices they kept in their cellars.

Everyone started eating and enjoying all that was provided. The children even ate their fill and enjoyed themselves. It didn't take long for the people of the village to sit back with satisfied grins on their faces. The eating was winding down and dessert was being served. There were special family recipes for cakes and pies and other specialties. It was heaven on earth.

It was voted by Aribon that after the main meal was cleaned up that they could all go home and rest to get ready for the dance later on. Everyone got up from the table and began to clean everything up. There were very few leftovers to take home or share, but they did share, especially the meat that was still left cooking. Aribon kept a lot of it for guests staying with him. Zarcon's group would be there for a while yet.

Zarcon was still healing and no one knew how long he would need to recover. Greta brought him some food and they ate together. She was still concerned about him and wanted him to stay in his room for a while longer.

Magg and Matton stayed in her room in the inn. Matton brought them both a large plate of food. Magg needed it to replace all she had lost using her magic during the battle with Neberon. They ate their fill and enjoyed the time alone together.

Donavan and Jasmine had joined the villagers at the tables. They had many friends in the village and wanted to visit and share experiences of the past few weeks. There was much to share.

Jarrone and his family had their own table near the rest of the villagers. There were many who came over and thanked Jarrone for his help in the battle of magic. They were very grateful for all he had done, eventhough he didn't realize how important his part in it really was. Neberon had made him feel small.

His father and siblings were really enjoying the food and the people. They were making many friends this day. There was even a widow in the village that took a liking to their father. Only time would tell if anything developed beyond friendship there.

After eating and cleaning up the area and moving the tables to the outside edges of the village green, the benches were set in a circle to prepare for the dancing. When all was accomplished, the people all agreed that it was time to rest until time for the dancing. What a great day so far with more fun to come.

CHAPTER 19

MAGG AND MATTON

M AGG AND MATTON had stayed in her room that day. Magg was too worn out from the magic she had used against Neberon to consider joining all the other people in the celebration. She was kind of sad to miss it, but she just couldn't handle any people just now. Matton was such a comfort and held her most of the day.

As the day wore on and they were still alone, Magg started to feel better. Matton leaned over and kissed her. Magg responded with longing. Soon enough, their clothes were off and they made passionate love to one another. It was so gentle and sweet that it was all Magg could do, not to moan and nearly cry out with pleasure. Matton was so gentle and kind, it really kindled Magg's passion.

So she said, "Could we do that again?"

Matton just smiled and kissed her again. That was all it took.

Later, they could hear the villagers and Donavan and Jasmine talking. It sounded like they were coming close to Magg's room. She jumped up and Matton, too. They threw on their clothes just as Donavan yelled at them. "Hey, are you two ever coming out? The dancing is about to start. Besides, Magg, you're the celebrity of the hour and everyone is asking about you.

We've missed you and Matton all day. Come and have some fun. Nap time is officially over."

Jasmine giggled at that. She was suspicious of both of them. She had a pretty good idea of what was going on in Magg's room all day. So, it was when Magg and Matton finally opened the door, they were met with two smiling faces. They were both a little embarrassed, but hey, it was fun.

The thing about it was that Donavan and Jasmine had been doing the same thing the past two hours. That was why Jasmine got such a giggle about it.

The four of them finally headed to the town square and joined the celebration. When Magg and Matton walked into the square, the crowd began to applaud Magg for saving them all from Neberon. Magg was embarrassed again, but she appreciated the gratitude of the villagers.

They started yelling, "SPEECH, SPEECH!!"

Magg refused, but they insisted. Even Jasmine and Donavan chimed in.

So, Magg decided she'd better say something, "Thank you! I just want to say that with the help of Zarcon, Donavan, and Jarrone, we were able to stop the evil that was Neberon. None of us could have done it alone. I'm so grateful that no one was hurt badly. It was a terrible thing to have to fight with magic. One can never be too sure of the outcome. We were very lucky to have had things go our way. It could have so easily gone the other way. Enough of that! Let's dance and have some fun right now!"

At that, the band started to play and everyone found a partner and started dancing. Jarrone had joined the group with his siblings. Hoskins came too. It was so nice to do something fun as brothers and sisters. It seemed a long while since they had been able to have any fun at all.

Revinia and Lucintha had worn pretty dresses and were ready to dance. Jarrone was hoping he would find a girl to dance with. Hoskins seemed lost in his own little world. It was hoped that he would join the fun soon.

It wasn't long before a handsome young man asked Revinia to dance. Lucintha was asked soon after. They danced and danced. It was truly the most fun they had had in a long time.

Dessert was served again with lots of punch, ale, wine, and homemade beer for one and all. The band was wonderful even though they hit an off key once in a while. No one cared in the least.

Jarrone finally asked a young lady, Coreen, to dance after looking the girls over. She was blond with freckles across her nose and a big smile. He asked her to dance and she eagerly said yes. They talked and got to know each other while they were dancing and having a great time.

Jarrone walked her over to the dessert table where they each decided what they would like to eat. Both drank some spring water. Dessert was great. Jarrone was hoping he could visit Coreen after the dance, maybe in a couple of days. He even asked her if it would be alright if he did. She smiled and nodded, too happy to say anything.

Revinia and Lucintha were dancing with a different boy almost every dance. They were having the time of their lives.

Hoskins finally decided he would join in the group dancing. He was too young to dance with a girl. He felt too uncomfortable at the idea of it. But he had a great time with the group dances. The older folks were helping him get the steps and he loved it.

Magg and Matton danced most of the time, but Magg was getting tired so they decided to sit out a few dances. Matton brought her some dessert and some red wine. It was such a nice evening together. Magg was truly happy.

Donavan and Jasmine were having a great time dancing every dance and visiting with the villagers. They got to know so many of them. They knew most of them because of the effort of helping them recover from the Black Wind. Now that all that was in the past, they could finally enjoy the relationships formed.

CHAPTER 20

ZARCON

G RETA WAS WITH Zarcon. He wasn't doing very well. His wound was not healing. She was concerned that it might get infected. So, she stayed with him and talked about old times. It had been a long time since they had any time to do that. They had been so busy with all that was going on since they got to Anakik. Now, things were finally settled a bit and they could relax together.

Donavan and Jasmine came to see Zarcon later in the evening before he went to sleep.

"How are you doing, Zarcon?"

"I'm feeling a little better, but this darn wound just won't heal all the way like it should. Do you think Magg could come and look at it, maybe tomorrow?"

Jasmine replied, "Of course, Zarcon. I'll even see if she's up to seeing you tonight. I'll let you know. Would that be alright?"

"I would surely appreciate anything you can do. It's hurting me lately. Greta has helped keep me calm, but I'm concerned."

"I understand why. Donavan and I will go see her right away."

At that, they both left to find Magg. They had last seen her on the chairs close to the firepit. It didn't take long to figure out where she was. As soon as they saw Matton, they knew where Magg was.

"Magg! How are you doing tonight? Are you up to taking a look at Zarcon? He's concerned that his wound isn't healing like it should. He's saying that it hurts now."

Magg was suddenly concerned, "Of course, I'll come. Anything I can do I will do."

Matton followed Magg to Zarcon's room. As soon as she saw him, she knew he wasn't doing well. When she walked in, Zarcon smiled. He was so glad to see her. He knew that if anyone could help him, it would be Magg.

"Zarcon, how are you feeling? I understand you're concerned about your wound. Can I look at it for a minute?"

"Of course, maybe you can tell me what's going on. It's odd that wizards can't heal themselves. It's very aggravating."

Magg removed the bandages and looked at the wound. It had been caused by Neberon's spell when he cast red glass at them. A small piece of it happened to hit Zarcon.

"Zarcon, why didn't you call me sooner?"

"I knew you would be so worn out from all the magic yesterday with Neberon. I know I was, and I didn't do half of what you did."

"I don't care, you're more important than that. This isn't good. I'm going to have to use magic on it. Is that alright?"

"Yes, you know I trust you."

Magg drew on her magic and entered Zarcon where his wound was. She could sense that it was festering even though she had tried to heal it before. Greta had put some herbs on it that had probably kept it from getting any worse than it was. But it wasn't healing like it should, even considering Zarcon's age.

Magg went deeper into Zarcon's system and found the problem. There was a strange organism that was mutating and messing up his body. It was now throughout his bodily organs and was busy destroying them. She tried to destroy the organism, but it had taken over. She could heal some of the damage, but she couldn't cure him. There was something about the piece of red glass that must have had the organism all over it.

Magg went deep into her magic to find the cure, but this was not something she could do anything with. It was then that she realized Zarcon had been ordained to die. With great sorrow, she withdrew the magic and looked at Zarcon. He knew as soon as she looked at him what it meant. She couldn't heal him and he was dying.

Greta sensed it too. She started crying softly and started to leave the room so Zarcon wouldn't see her cry. She didn't want to upset him. But he called her back.

"Greta, why do you want to leave me now? I need you more than ever. Please, please, stay with me."

Greta came back realizing her mistake. She was thinking of herself instead of what Zarcon needed at that moment. She was still crying softly. But she laid next to Zarcon and held him. She sent all the comforting feelings to him that she could. He seemed to calm down a bit. He had been aging fast the last few months and knew he probably wouldn't live much longer. But this was something else. His life was being cut short by some evil creature and his evil magic. It made him angry for a bit. But he relaxed and decided that it was what it was meant to be. He couldn't do anything to change it now and anger would only make it worse for him.

As Zarcon thought more about it, he remembered thinking that if he could help with the fight against Neberon before he died, he would be grateful. He had helped and it now cost him his life. But he truly was grateful for the chance he had to help rid the land of the evil that was Neberon. Maybe that was his reason for living this long. He needed to see the end of Neberon. Was this meant to remind him of something? He thought about it some more.

His friends gathered around him when they heard the news of his condition. It was breaking everyone's heart. He finally just said, "Look! I'm not dead yet!"

As sad as they were, they started to laugh. Zarcon could be funny when he half tried, but this time he was only half kidding. However, he had relaxed the situation for everyone. It was decided that they would enjoy every minute left to him and Zarcon was glad.

Suddenly, Zarcon had an idea he hoped the others would like.

"Listen everyone, I have an idea. What if we started a school for wizards and anyone with magic of any kind? What do you think?"

Donavan spoke first, "Zarcon! That's a great idea! Why didn't we think of it before? There is a rich history of the schools for wizards throughout the study of magic. Of course, there is a certain risk involved, but maybe we could set boundaries or something to protect the people from another Neberon. What do the rest of you think?"

Magg replied, "Sounds like a great idea. Where and when would we start such a thing? There is so much to consider. Should we have a meeting with everyone that might be involved, and make a plan and get started? But again, where and when would that be? I vote that it be soon so that Zarcon can help with the planning."

"He knows what's involved. He was in a school for wizards for years, right, Zarcon?"

Zarcon looked at Magg and with a smile said, "I was and I know much about the workings of one. It would be my honor to help plan one of our own. I saw many problems with the one I was in. So, hopefully, I could help avoid them, or at least most of them."

Everyone was in agreement with the plan to get started and have Zarcon help in any way he could. But there was still the issue of when and where? There was some talk about staying in Anakik. Others wanted to go back to Synkana.

Jarrone spoke up, "Maybe we could use my village of Solvig. It's small, but that might be a good thing. We'd have plenty of room to build the school and it would be out of the way of the big cities where we could have some privacy and others with magic could come to us without being afraid of the city people. I'm just suggesting."

"It looks like we have some options now," Magg said. "Let's talk about the planning meeting. Where do we want to have that? We could go to any of the cities or villages suggested."

"I would like to have the planning meeting here. I'm not sure Zarcon would want to wait until we get to Synkana. Solvig isn't far, but the road there isn't the greatest. Any other ideas?"

After some silent thought, it was decided that the meeting would indeed be held there in Anakik. That way, Zarcon wouldn't need to be moved and they could get started right away. It was agreed that they would meet in Zarcon's room the next morning. Everyone was tired after their eventful day. So they left for their own rooms and went to bed.

Greta stayed with Zarcon in case he needed anything. She also wanted to comfort him and herself by being close to him. Finally, Zarcon drifted off to sleep and spent a comfortable night with Greta.

Magg said she needed Matton to stay with her again. She was feeling lonely and he agreed to spend another night with her. They were quickly falling in love and wanted to be together every minute.

Donavan and Jasmine noticed their feelings for each other growing as time went by. It was exciting to know that Magg had such a man as Matton in love with her. He seemed to give her strength when she needed it. The thought struck them that maybe he could be an empath like Greta. That would be wonderful. The two of them would be great together and help the school they were planning immeasurably.

Jarrone went back to his family. They stayed in one of the houses that were left vacant after it was repaired when the Black Wind came. The family that lived there were killed by the mist monsters. No one told them that, however. It was such a sad story that no one spoke of it.

He told his family about the school for wizards and anyone who had magic. He was so excited. Now, he would be able to find out what his magic really was. Revinia felt the same way. Hoskins didn't seem to care. Lucintha thought she probably didn't have any magic, so she didn't care either. But their father was excited about it just because his son and daughter were.

His father asked if they would have to move away from Solvig. Jarrone didn't know that yet. They were to meet the next morning and talk about it.

It was getting late, so the family went to bed for the night.

The next morning came early. All those with magic were excited to go to the meeting to discuss the new wizard school they wanted to start. Zarcon had slept soundly with Greta there to comfort him. He was grateful the meeting would be held in his room as he wasn't much for going anywhere. His wound was bothering him now that he was awake.

Aribon, the innkeeper, brought a large table for them to sit around. He had chairs for everyone ready to be taken to Zarcon's room. As the group arrived, Aribon showed them the chairs and they each took one. Zarcon's room was one of the largest guest rooms at the inn. It was perfect for the meeting that was about to start.

Magg and Matton came in first, then Donavan and Jasmine, Jarrone and his sister, Revinia, came in last. They found places for their chairs and gathered around the table. Zarcon was able to sit in one of the chairs with Greta next to him. It was a solemn group that met that morning. It was important and they were all beginning to feel it. They were glad Zarcon could join them at the table.

Zarcon started the meeting saying, "You all know why we're here. We have much to discuss. I would like to start by making a suggestion for a person to head the wizard school. I have thought about it since the day I decided a wizard school would be a good thing. I want to suggest that Magg be the head of the school. Magg, I know I didn't talk to you about this, but you really are needed. You have the strongest magic and the most control of it. You have much to teach the others who might want to learn from you and Donavan. Do you have an answer?"

Magg was caught off guard by the question and wasn't sure what to think. Matton squeezed her hand and smiled in reassurance. That was all she needed, she said, "Zarcon, if you think that is the best place for me to serve, I accept the invitation."

Everyone around the table applauded her decision. She was the most likely person for the position. She was so powerful that no one else came close to what she could do. It would be good to have one so powerful to be the leader. Magg looked around at all the smiling faces and felt such warmth from them. She knew then that she had made the right decision.

Zarcon then said, "Now that that is out of the way, let's talk about where we want to have the school. Three places have been suggested, Synkana, Solvig, and Anakik. Does anyone have other ideas?" He let them think about it for a few minutes. When no one else said anything, Zarcon said, "I have my own idea, but let's vote on the place to start. Write your choice on the papers I had Aribon bring each of you. Greta will count them for us."

As the papers were handed in, Greta took them and started counting the choices. Surprisingly, the place most of them wanted to have the school was Synkana. Zarcon nodded. "That is where I wanted it to be as well. But I didn't want to sway any of you. Why do you think Synkana would be best? Let's start with Magg."

"I thought about Synkana because it's a major city and would draw more potential people with magic. There's a lot of places we could build the school on or buy a building that's already there. I like that idea best. We can start small and then expand as needed."

Donavan spoke next, "I voted for Synkana because we spent a lot of time there and found the people to be accepting of magic. I also agree with Magg about the city. In the smaller villages, we would have to start from scratch and that could be expensive."

Jarrone wanted to say a few words next, "I voted for Solvig because it is out of the way and quiet. I think the villagers would be happy to help us build the school. It wouldn't cost much if they do and we could get exactly what we want. Also, maybe the people of Synkana are alright with magic now, but what if their mood changes? You know how people are? What if they turned against us someday? What then? From what I've learned from my mother's Book of Spells, most wizarding schools were in secluded places not in big cities. It makes me a bit nervous to think of it being in Synkana. But I will go along with whatever is decided by the group."

Zarcon thought about what Jarrone had said, "Jarrone, you have brought up things I hadn't even thought about. In so many ways, you're right. Let's have another vote. Jarrone has some good reasons for choosing a smaller village."

Aribon brought in more papers for them. He had been waiting outside the door in case he was needed. They took another vote and Greta gathered the papers up and counted them again. She gave the numbers to Zarcon. Zarcon looked up in surprise. "It looks like you've all changed your mind thanks to Jarrone. I'm sorry, Jarrone, it isn't Solvig, but Anakik that has been voted for the school. Now, who wants to tell me why that is?"

Jarrone was thinking about why that was. He said, "I think I know part of the reason. You all have good feelings about Anakik. You've grown attached to the wonderful people here. You've helped them a lot and this village is special. I've felt that too. Plus, I know these people would be more than happy to build us a school. They obviously are not afraid of magic since it saved their lives and helped them heal from all they've dealt with here for the past year. I like it here, I just wanted to be home in Solvig.

But we're close enough and Anakik is just a bit bigger, not like Synkana. What I'm trying to say is, Anakik it is for me too."

"Now that we have that settled, let's figure out when we want to start the school. How soon do you think we could get the materials and help we'll need to get building?" Zarcon was so happy that they were going to build in Anakik. Now, he could watch the progress and be a small part of it all. He hugged Greta after everyone left. It felt good to be near her. He knew she would be his comfort for however long he had left of life.

As everyone was leaving, they chatted about the new thing that was going to happen right there in Anakik. Aribon was listening and it made him happy too. He had grown very fond of these people who came and saved his village and helped rebuild it from the destruction of the Black Wind. He also knew that the other villagers felt the same way. The celebration they had just enjoyed proved that. For the first time in many years, there was a spirit of joy here and it was wonderful.

Jarrone and Revinia left the meeting feeling happier than they had felt in a while. They couldn't wait to tell their father about what had been decided. Jarrone was also excited that he had been a part of the decision. Life was shaping up to be very interesting and exciting at the same time.

CHAPTER 21

THE BOYS MEET ANDORON

ROSLIN WANTED THE boys to meet Andoron before they left Solvig. So, she set up a meeting at her home. She invited Andoron to have dinner with the family that night. Roslin cooked a great meal for them and when Andoron knocked on the door, she invited him in. He had cleaned himself up and looked nice enough. Dinner went well with talk about Anakik and how they would get there and how long it would take.

Andoron said, "I'm thinking we'll be there in about a day and a half. There's a trail we can take that is narrow and rocky, but it's the fastest way there. We'll camp for the night in the forest and move on early the next day. We should be in Anakik by late afternoon."

"I'll have food for myself if the boys can have food enough for themselves, we'll be good to get there by then. It should be uneventful as we travel. It seems that Neberon scared the big animals away. They'll be back, but hopefully not right away."

Kedron was unsure about going with him. He had a funny feeling about him. But he decided that if Roslin was fine with them going with this man, he must be alright. So he ignored his feelings and went along hoping they would be with Zarcon by late afternoon of the next day.

For his part, Andoron played the nice man while living in Solvig. He had not been there very long, almost a year. Just long enough for the villagers to think of him as being kind. He could play the part that long. But now, it was wearing thin and he needed an excuse to get out of Solvig.

When Neberon had come to the village seeking Jarrone, he felt the evil in that creature. He had stayed in his house while Neberon passed through, but he knew the power Neberon had was something he wanted desperately. He could feel it as he passed by his door. As he thought about Neberon, he realized the creature had to have a cave or place he lived in. Andoron wanted to find that place. Maybe he could find the Book of Spells Neberon used. He knew he had some magic, but he didn't have any idea how to use it. If he found this Book of Spells, he would soon find out all he needed to know. He would use the boys as an excuse to get out of town and stay out.

When Roslin came to the village store asking if anyone were planning on going to Anakik and wouldn't mind taking two boys with him, he jumped at the chance. He just needed two days to gather all the equipment he would need for their "trip".

No one seemed to notice all the odd things he bought the next two days before he planned on leaving. He purchased a long knife, pliers, a rope, bandanas, jerky, canteens, fishing gear, and hooks. None of the things he bought were suspicious to the store owner. Anyone else would think he was being prepared for a trip, not knowing he would be taking the two boys and only for a couple of days.

If Roslin had seen the things Andoron was buying, she might have become suspicious. But unfortunately, she wasn't there at the time. Most of the villagers of Solvig were very trusting and suspected nothing evil on the part of Andoron. Sadly, they would soon learn the cost of such naivete. They had dealt with evil in Neberon, but not with someone who was part of their village. It was something they could not imagine.

Boren and Kedron spent their last day in Solvig playing with Roslin's two boys. They ate with the family and really enjoyed their time together. Roslin and Karmine were very kind and helped them get ready to leave the next morning.

"Boren, Kedron, I have packed some clothes for both of you and in the morning I will pack food for your trip to Anakik. The man, Andoron, will be here early to take you with him, but I'll help you get ready to leave."

Kedron said, "Roslin, do you know Andoron well? Is he a good man? Will we be safe with him?"

"What's wrong, Kedron? Are you having second thoughts about leaving? Andoron has lived in Solvig for almost a year. He has been kind the entire time. We have grown to trust him, if that's what worries you."

Kedron shrugged his shoulders. He didn't know what to say or how to express his feelings on the matter. Boren caught a look on Kedron's face that scared him a little. He knew then that they would have to keep an eye on this man, Andoron. Maybe Kedron sensed something the rest of them had missed. Then again, maybe he was just being silly after all they had been through with Zedoc. Surely, they would be safe until they reached Zarcon.

The boys did not sleep well that night. They were excited to be with Zarcon soon, yet concerned about Andoron. Would he take good care of them? Or would he be another evil man who would hurt them or take them someplace they didn't want to go? Kedron was especially worried, but he didn't want Boren to think he was crazy so he kept his fears to himself.

The day finally came for Boren and Kedron to leave Solvig and go with Andoron. They were up early with Roslin loading their packs and putting some bread and cheese in a wrapper for their meals. She also added some carrots and apples. Karmine and their sons came to see them off. Boren and Kedron were both hugged goodbye. They all had tears in their eyes even though the boys wouldn't be going that far away.

Karmine was curious as to why there was such a reaction to them leaving. It shouldn't have been so sad. He surely hoped it held no sign of things to come. It was difficult for the boys to leave Roslin and Karmine. They had been so kind to them. They had also been good friends with their two sons. Now, they would be leaving and hoping to see Zarcon in a couple of days. The future held promise for them, but they were going into the unknown with a man they did not know.

Andoron showed up shortly after the boys were ready. He was all smiles and happy to see the boys. He helped them get their things on the horse. When both of them were on the horse and ready to leave, Andoron motioned for them to follow him. Roslin and Karmine waved them goodbye. It was hard to watch them go. The boys were so much a part of their family in such a short period of time. Roslin's sons cried when they were leaving the village.

Kedron was suddenly afraid of Andoron. He looked back at Roslin and Karmine with such a sad look on his face that Roslin almost stopped them from leaving. But she discounted her feelings and let them go hoping she wouldn't regret it.

As the three of them started into the forest on the trail Andoron followed, Kedron held onto Boren so tight that he protested, "Kedron, I can't breathe! Give me a little space, alright?"

Reluctantly, Kedron eased his grip, but he was still terrified and was on the verge of tears. Andoron had no idea Kedron was in such a state of anxiety. It's probably a good thing. Who knows what he would have done if he had known. The real Andoron was yet to reveal himself.

The trail narrowed and became rocky. They made slow progress as a result. The trees and brush were close to the trail and a few times a stray limb almost knocked the boys off their horse. It seemed that Andoron knew all of the hazards because he was always able to dodge the limbs before they got too close.

They were going along at a steady pace when Andoron stopped suddenly and told them they must take a different trail as there was a problem up ahead that made it impossible to keep going. So, it was then that they turned off the trail to take another less noticeable one, heading west this time. Kedron tried to tell Boren not to go that way, but he wouldn't listen.

"Andoron knows what he's doing, we need to follow him so we don't get lost."

"But Boren, I have a really bad feeling about going this way. It just doesn't feel right."

"You're just being silly. If Roslin and Karmine say Andoron is a good man, we have to trust their judgement, understand?"

"But Boren, what if they're wrong?"

At that moment, Andoron turned around as if he heard what was being said. He gave Kedron a dirty look and said, "Keep up, we have far to go and I won't have you slowing me down, got it?"

Boren suddenly saw what had so frightened Kedron. He whispered, "I think maybe I should have listened to you. It's too late to turn back now."

Kedron started crying again. He knew things weren't going to be good. He also had a terrible feeling he wouldn't even get to see Zarcon or any of his friends. That old feeling of despair hit him again. It seemed Boren might now be feeling the same way.

After another two hours of riding, Andoron called a halt to their ride. "Get off your horse, we're going to rest here a few moments and eat something. Then we'll be off again quickly. We do have far to go. I hope you have enough food for both of you. If not, you'll just have to go without." At that he gave them an evil smile. It was truly frightening. The real Andoron was finally showing himself.

The boys got down from their horse and opened their pack. They agreed to only eat a small amount of food for now. They wanted to make sure they would have enough for this trip to who knows where. They only drank a bit of the water from their canteens. They weren't sure of being able to fill them up again. It was sinking in that they were at the mercy of another evil man.

When they finished eating what little they chose to eat, Andoron came to them and said, "Now that you know more about me and what's really going on, I'm going to have to tie your hands so you can't run away. I will also hold your horse's reins so that you can't escape that way either. I wouldn't want that to happen when we're just getting to know each other, now would I?"

He tied their hands and lifted them up onto their horse. He threw their pack up with them. He gathered their horse's reins and pulled them over to his horse while he climbed up. He kicked his horse into a fast walk. The boys had a really tough time staying on their horse. It was difficult to hold onto anything with their hands tied so tight.

Andoron finally slowed the pace and kept moving. It was easier to stay on the horse, but not any more comfortable.

Andoron was planning on taking the boys to find Neberon's cave where he was hoping to practice the spells he was going to learn, on them. Plus, he had many implements of torture he had bought in Solvig. The boys were probably not going to live long once he got them there, but he needed them to practice on. He had big plans to do what Neberon had failed to do. He would destroy others with magic so that he could take over the world. He had really high hopes.

What he did not know was that the boys had dealt with an evil man before and knew some tricks of their own. They also hoped that Roslin and Karmine would find out they never got to Anakik and start searching for them soon. So as they traveled, Kedron left markers of which way they were being taken. Surely someone would find them before it was too late.

Boren and Kedron were miserable. Andoron kept going for far too long. The boys were about to fall off their horse from exhaustion and hunger. But since Andoron was feeling just fine, he didn't think to stop. After another hour of riding, Kedron really did fall off the horse and Boren could do nothing to stop him.

Kedron lay on the ground moaning. He was in pain from the fall and so tired and hungry he could hardly move at this point. Andoron heard him fall off the horse and stopped to see what was going on. When he saw Kedron on the ground, he was angry.

"What are you doing, you lazy boy? We have too far to go for you to decide to lay around napping. Get up! Get back on the horse so we can keep going!"

It gradually became apparent even to one as stupid as Andoron that Kedron wasn't faking. He also noticed that Boren was about to do the same. So Andoron jumped off his horse and pulled Boren from his horse and set him next to Kedron. He untied their hands so they could eat.

"Now, it looks like you two lazy boys need a rest or something. I will let you rest long enough to eat a bite of food and have some water. Then we'll be back at it, got that?"

Boren tried to get Kedron to sit up to eat, but he was so tired, he couldn't do it. So Boren pulled him over to a tree that was close by and leaned him up against it so he could eat something. He gave Kedron some cheese and bread and a carrot. He ate the same thing. But he ate slowly so Kedron would have more time to rest and finish his food. Boren was worried about Kedron. He seemed so small and frail. He hadn't noticed it before.

Andoron was losing patience, but let them eat in peace. He was pretty sure he was on the right path because he could see the remains of the passage of Neberon. There were many small animals that he had killed. He also saw where the villagers had been killed. He had more and more respect for Neberon as he rode along. He was so powerful and had no conscience to be able to kill so many living things. He wanted to be just as evil himself. He still had a little bit of a conscience, but he was losing it quick enough. He was sure he could be even better and more powerful than Neberon. He was a dreamer full of himself and his dreams. But would he be able to realize any of them? Would he rule the world someday? Not if he didn't get these two boys moving soon.

"Come on, you two! Time's wasting. We only have a couple more hours before dark. We must keep moving, so get up and let's go!"

Boren was feeling a little better, but Kedron could barely speak, let alone ride. Andoron came over to tie their hands again. He saw how tired Kedron was and doubted that he would be able to ride at all if he tied his hands. Boren didn't look much better. So he decided to let them go without being tied up. He was sure that they were both too tired to try anything this day.

Andoron lifted both boys onto their horse. He knew they couldn't do it alone. Then he took the reins of their horse and mounted his own horse and started off. He didn't go quite as fast as he had been. He knew if he didn't take care of the boys now, he wouldn't have them to practice on later. It was a small price to pay.

Boren was hating Andoron more by the minute. He knew he would kill this evil man as soon as he had the chance. He would not be able to hurt anyone else as he was hurting them now. He also feared there would be more hurt to come when they got to the place Andoron was taking them. He was trying to come up with the way to either escape this evil man or to destroy him.

Boren knew that Kedron had some magical power. The difficulty was that Kedron didn't believe it. In fact, that was part of why they were seeking Zarcon. Boren was hoping Zarcon could tell Kedron what magic he had. It really was obvious that Kedron had some form of magic when he seemed to know the spirit of a person. He also seemed able to sense the future if they kept going as they were.

The problem now, however, was how to get away from this situation. Boren tried to keep Kedron upright and awake. But Kedron was obviously exhausted and in need of a lot of rest to recover. He wasn't going to get enough as long as they were following Andoron.

The forest had thinned out now and they had started to climb a hill. The trees were sparse and the plants there were prickly with lots of sage brush and other weeds. The horses were having a difficult time after walking for so long. Now they must walk up a hill that was rocky and steep. The rocks were actually shale stones. It made climbing the hill treacherous.

Andoron seemed oblivious of all this. His horse was doing just as bad as Boren and Kedron's horse. Suddenly, Andoron's horse stumbled and nearly fell to his knees. Andoron was abruptly awakened to the situation.

"Well, well, it looks like the horses have had enough today. The problem is, we can't stop here. I'm thinking we'll have to get off our horses and walk them up this hill. Ready, boys?"

Boren was upset, "But Kedron is exhausted and he can't walk. Please let him stay on the horse and I will walk."

"You're quite the brother, aren't you? I don't care how you do it, as long as we get to the top of this hill today."

So, Boren told Kedron what was going on and then dismounted from his horse. He started walking the horse up the hill. The loose shale made progress on foot difficult. His horse did better now that they were going a lot slower. Boren kept slipping and nearly fell several times.

Andoron was sliding as well. He kept going, but he was even having a difficult time hiking up the hill. The progress of Andoron and Boren was very slow. It felt as though they were taking two steps forward and one or two steps back.

Not only was the shale loose, it was also sharp. If anyone fell or if one of the horses fell, the result could be a disaster. As it was, the horses were at risk of having one of their hooves cut by the shale. Boren kept praying to the gods that none of that would happen. Right now, the top seemed miles away.

As it turned out, Neberon's cave was at the end of the next hill. However, that hill was steeper and the shale was harder to get through. Neberon had been riding Negra, so he didn't have to touch the shale. Negra could rise above the ground when he wanted to. This, of course, was not an option for Andoron and Boren.

Andoron was beginning to feel the magic of Neberon's cave. He knew he was getting close. The sun had come up bright and the sky was a beautiful blue. He took it as a sign that he would find the cave and get all that magic from Neberon's Book of Spells. He was grateful that he had two victims to practice on. It would be so much more rewarding for him that way.

The two of them that were hiking were able to barely keep moving. It was getting late and both Andoron and Boren were becoming exhausted. They couldn't go much farther. As a matter of fact, they finally found a shelf off their trail that had an overhang. It was free of shale and looked to have been swept. It was just a bit higher on the hill. They kept going and finally made it. Andoron made it first and collapsed. Boren did the same. Kedron was still on the horse and not happy that he had been left there.

"Boren, did you forget about me? Please! Help me down from this horse. My body hurts all over!"

Boren was barely able to get back up and walk over to Kedron. He was just able to catch him as he basically fell off the horse. Boren helped him walk to the shelf and they both laid down and fell asleep on the hard ground.

They slept in spite of the hard ground and the heat from the sun on them. Fortunately, they were at a higher altitude and so the heat was not as bad as in the valley below. It was getting dark when they finally woke up. Andoron decided if they wouldn't make any progress now, it was too late. So, gratefully, they spent the night there. They were able to eat what they had and relax the whole evening and they slept that night.

All seemed quiet and they slept well. However, there was a reason the area seemed to have been swept. It wasn't a good reason. There were creatures that had been created by Neberon that used it for a trap for any humans foolish enough to stop there. Not many did because of the difficulty getting there. But when humans did stop there, there were usually more than one. That meant that more of them could eat. They now saw that there was a large male human and two smaller ones. That would be plenty for the next few days if they were careful.

They were creeping up on the three sleeping humans even then. They were long-limbed and thin of body. They were slightly humanoid in appearance, but their eyes were much too big for their heads. Their eyes gave off an eerie red light, much like Neberon's eyes. He had created them when he was bored and before he slept. He enjoyed creating things that were dangerous, such as the mist monsters. He hadn't turned these creatures loose on humanity, but he just enjoyed creating them.

Andoron was about to find them a bit close for comfort.

CHAPTER 22

ZARCON AND GRETA II

ZARCON SEEMED TO be failing faster now. Greta could comfort him, but it was becoming increasingly difficult. He was getting to the point that the pain had increased and he needed something more to calm him. Finally, he asked for Magg to come help him. He was hoping she could do something for the pain.

Magg suspected that Zarcon would need her to stop the pain if she could. She had been resting in case the magic was intense. She had no way of knowing. As she walked to Zarcon's room, she kept thinking about what she could do to help him now that the pain was worse. As she entered his room, she could see that he really was failing faster than she had hoped.

Zarcon tried to smile when she came, but couldn't do it. He said, "Thank you for coming, Magg. I'm really hurting. Greta's herbs aren't doing much anymore. Will you try to help me?"

Magg replied, "Of course, Zarcon, it would be my honor to do anything I can to help you." Magg touched Zarcon and searched for a way to stop the pain. She finally found the nerves that were inflamed. She decided she might as well sever them. It would stop the pain, but it might leave some small part of his body numb. It didn't seem like it would be a bad thing.

Zarcon sighed when she took care of the nerves. He was finally without pain. He was amazed. "Magg, what have you done? You've stopped the pain and I feel good for once."

"Zarcon, if the pain comes back, which I'm thinking it won't, please come and get me immediately, alright?"

"I surely will, Magg. Now that I know something can be done about it. Thank you, my dear friend."

Magg had tears in her eyes knowing she had helped Zarcon who was in so much pain. Now she knew how to stop intense pain when someone was at the end of their life. She felt good about what she had done. She hoped that the pain would not return. Zarcon really was a dear friend. He had taught her much about magic when she finally found him what seemed like years ago. Oh, the times they had been through together and with the others. She could never have expected that her life would be so full back then. Magg gave Zarcon and Greta a hug and said goodbye for now.

Magg was so grateful that now she had Matton to love and be loved. It amazed her now after looking back on her life. She was so grateful that Zora had died so she could find her life without her. She had been so mean to Magg that it hurt her. But she would not dwell on that, it was in the past and no longer mattered.

She left her room and went to find Matton. He was just outside the inn waiting for her. He wanted to go for a long walk to talk about his feelings for her. He wanted her to know exactly what he was feeling and what he wanted from their relationship.

Magg sensed that it was important to Matton. So, she went with him to a trail in the forest that wound around Anakik to a beautiful waterfall they had found on a previous walk there. They finally sat on a broad flat rock to talk. It was so beautiful there with the waterfall and ferns and water flowers growing between the rocks in random places on the rock wall. The sun was shining through the leaves of the nearby trees and speckled the water droplets with light.

Matton was nervous. He loved Magg with all his heart, yet she was so powerful it was a little bit scary for him to talk to her the way he wanted to. He finally said, "Magg, I have some things to tell you. First, I love you more than I can say. Second, I want you in my life for the rest of my life. Third, my dear Magg, will you please marry me?"

Magg started to cry, "Matton, I thought you'd never ask. I have loved you dearly for so long, almost since the first day I saw you. You've been there for me no matter what and given me strength and courage to be me. I owe the best part of who I am to you. Of course, I'll marry you!" She hugged and kissed him passionately.

Of course, that was all it took. One thing led to another and they were on the grass making love in that beautiful setting. They lay together for a while and finally fell asleep in each other's arms. Neither one of them fit the mold for beauty, but they were so in love it didn't matter.

Finally, they woke up and put their clothes back on. They laid back down together and talked about their future and made some plans. It was a wonderful day. They walked back to the village hand in hand, glowing with the love they felt for each other. It was obvious to anyone who cared to look that they were madly in love and so happy together.

As they entered Anakik, they decided they'd better check on Zarcon. He was in peril right now and might need Magg to help him with his pain. They walked to the inn and to Zarcon's room.

Greta was there with him, holding him. She smiled when they walked in. She whispered, "Zarcon is sleeping. He's not had so much pain today. Thank you, Magg, for your help. He really appreciates what you did for him the today. He's been able to sleep since then. He doesn't eat much, but when he does eat, it stays down. All good things, right?"

"Very good things. I came to see if he needed anything, but it sounds like he's doing alright. Please call me the minute he does need something. I'll keep checking in on him as well. By the way, how are you doing, Greta? Do you need a break or anything else? Could we bring you something to eat?"

Greta was so grateful for Magg's concern. She said, "Magg, I would love something to eat. I've been here with Zarcon so long and I don't dare leave him for very long. So as a result, I haven't eaten for a while."

"What could we bring you, dear? I'm sure Aribon would fix anything you could want."

"You're so kind, Magg. I would really like some of Aribon's stew and bread with a cup of wine, please."

"We'll be right back with your food."

Magg was sad to think no one had thought much about Greta having needs. She said, "Matton, I'm half angry that we didn't think of Greta before now. She's been an angel and never complains or asks for anything for herself. I could cry."

"I agree, Magg. Let's hurry and talk to Aribon about what Greta wants to eat. Maybe we could get her something special while we're at it."

"What are you thinking, Matton? Like a new dress or something? I would like that for her. But let's talk to Aribon first, of course."

"Good idea."

So they went to the kitchen and asked Aribon for some stew for Greta.

"Of course, I have some made for today as a matter of fact." He prepared a tray for Greta and included some crusty bread and a flagon of wine.

"Thank you so much, Aribon, you are so generous!"

"Anything for Zarcon and his friends. Greta helped me through a tough time when my inn was being rebuilt. So, I owe her a lot."

"Just the same, we're very grateful."

Matton and Magg took the tray to Greta and stayed with Zarcon while she sat at the table to eat. He woke up a little when Greta left his bed, but went back to sleep. Magg checked him with magic just to see what was going on in his body. She found that the organism was still attacking his organs, but not as aggressively as before. She was hoping it was because of the treatment she had done to cut the pain nerves. Whatever it was, she was grateful for the extra time it would give Zarcon.

Greta said, "I'm so glad you brought me food. It's so good. Aribon was very generous. I might have enough to eat tomorrow." She had finished eating and was heading toward Zarcon to continue comforting him.

Magg replied, "Don't worry about that. We'll be back tomorrow to make sure you get more food. I'm so glad we could help you today. Matton and I are going to do a little shopping but we'll be back soon, alright?"

"Sure, it will be good to spend more time with you later."

"Bye for now."

Matton and Magg left to go talk to Jarrone's sister about a dress for Greta. They felt that she deserved something nice after all she'd done for Zarcon. They found her at home working in the yard planting flowers.

"Hi, Revinia, can we talk for a few minutes?"

"Sure." She walked over to Magg and Matton. She was really curious about what they might want from her.

99

"We've been thinking about Greta. She's been taking care of Zarcon and has really helped us in all our adventures the past year. We were wondering if you would be willing to make her a nice dress as a thank you? Would you be able to do that? We'll surely pay you for it, of course."

Revinia was excited to think they would want one of her dresses for Greta. She loved Greta. "I would be honored to do that for Greta. What color would you like it to be?"

"Revinia, you have such great style and ideas, we'll leave it to you. We're sure whatever you do, it will be beautiful. I think Greta is just a bit bigger than you right now. She hasn't been eating much until now."

"I know just what to do. She will be lovely. I'll have fun doing it for her."

"Let us know when it's ready or if you need any help, alright?"

"I will do that."

Magg and Matton walked out into the sunshine and headed for the dining hall for dinner.

They met Donavan and Jasmine on their way there, too. Magg told Jasmine about the dress she was having Revinia make for Greta.

"That's a great idea! She will love it. Can we help buy it with you? We would love to."

"Actually, we might need a bit of help. I'm not sure what it's going to cost. We'll let you know."

Donavan asked, "How is Zarcon doing? We will be visiting him after dinner."

"He's doing alright. He's been able to sleep and eat a little now. Greta is grateful. She doesn't have to put so much magic into him now to comfort him. It was wearing her out. She still lays by him and comforts him as much as she can. He really depends on her. But we have to remember to make sure she's eating. I'm afraid we've not taken very good care of her lately. We've been so worried about Zarcon."

"You're right. We have to take good care of Greta too. She's doing so much for Zarcon and neglecting her own needs. That's not good for either of them."

They had just arrived at the dining room of the inn. Revinia waved at them as they entered. So, they sat with Jarrone and his family at one of the bigger tables. It was good for them all to be together again. Dinner was the same stew Magg and Matton had taken to Greta. It was especially good. Aribon had baked his famous sourdough bread. He always had ale and beer and fresh water or juices.

When dinner was almost done he brought out the dessert. He had made some apple pie for everyone. As the guests ate the pie, it was voted the best ever. Aribon was learning to cook more and more types of food and doing a better job all the time. He found that he really did enjoy cooking and taking care of his guests. Desserts were a new thing for him and when he got such high praise for his apple pie, he decided he needed to do more of it. At the celebration, it was the women who brought the desserts. He was interested then to try it on his own. It made his life more interesting to try new things in the kitchen.

Aribon had a helper named Alfias who helped him in the kitchen. He did the dishes and helped clean up. He had been with Aribon for two years, but he was always in the kitchen and didn't interact with anyone but Aribon. He was large for his age and very shy. It seemed he was a bit afraid of people, especially girls. He was also quite good looking, but he didn't realize it because he never spoke with anyone but Aribon.

Aribon had been encouraging him to come out and talk to his guests, but he couldn't do it. Alfias stayed with his sister in the village, but she never went anywhere except shopping for food. Alfias mostly stayed home and rested from his work at the inn. He got the hard work that needed doing. He weeded the garden and brought in whatever Aribon needed while he was cooking. He swept and mopped the floors, cleaned the counters and stove. He put away the supplies as they arrived. He helped Aribon with anything heavy that needed lifting or moving.

The good thing about his job was that he could keep to himself. He didn't have to go out and chat with the guests like Aribon did. He was grateful. Then when Jarrone's family were eating dinner that night, Alfias happened to look out the door and see Revinia and Lucintha. He was afraid of Revinia, she was much too pretty. Lucintha was pretty, but in a softer way. He really wanted to go talk to her. She was probably too young to court, but so was he. He was hoping they might be friends.

Aribon saw Alfias looking at the girls and encouraged him to take a chance and go talk to them. Aribon offered to go with him and introduce him to the guests. Alfias decided that would be alright. So they both went to the table where the girls were sitting.

Aribon stepped up to them and said, "I would like you all to meet my kitchen helper. His name is Alfias and he's a hard worker and shy. That's why you've never seen him before. He's been hiding in my kitchen."

Everyone said, "Hello, Alfias." Revinia and Lucintha blushed. Alfias really was good looking. But he was also very young, not much older than Lucintha. The girls smiled at him and continued to blush. It was fun to watch the young people meeting each other. None of them knew what to say at first.

Finally, Lucintha said, "Do you want to join us for a minute? We could talk a little. Would that be alright, Aribon?"

"It would for just a few minutes, Alfias will need to help me clean up in a bit."

"Great, Alfias, you can sit here by me. Did you get some pie? You should get some and come here by me to eat it."

Alfias was embarrassed, but happy. He got a piece of pie and joined Lucintha at the table. Jarrone was watching him closely. He could see that Alfias was a good person. But he didn't want anyone courting his sister, Lucintha. Maybe they could be friends, but that would have to do until she was older.

So the two of them chatted for a few minutes getting to know one another until Alfias had to go help Aribon in the kitchen. He left with a bit of a smile on his face.

The girls were so happy that Alfias had come to talk to them. He was so nice and would make a great friend for Lucintha. After dinner, they went back home feeling really happy about the day.

CHAPTER 23

ANDORON☒S END

A NDORON WAS HAPPY that they were almost to Neberon's cave. He could feel it. As he tried to sleep, he felt something strange was nearby. He knew Neberon had created the monsters in the mist, but he hadn't thought about him creating other possible creatures. He stirred and looked out into the blackness. That's when he saw the red eyes watching them. He jumped up and tried to run for his horse. He didn't bother to warn the boys, that was their problem now. But as he made for his horse, the creatures attacked him. They were attracted to movement and he moved first. He started screaming when the first monster bit his leg and pulled him down to the ground.

Fortunately, he woke up the boys. They could see that Andoron was being attacked by some strange creatures. They both crawled off the shelf and made for their horse. The creatures didn't seem to notice them as they stayed low and moved slowly. When they got close to their horse, they ran for it. Boren got up on the horse and pulled Kedron up. They took off before the creatures realized what was happening.

The creatures were content with Andoron. He was big and would feed all of them. The boys were small and wouldn't amount to much of a meal. So, they let them go and enjoyed Andoron to the fullest. He had stopped screaming and died a terrible death just short of Neberon's cave. It was then that they saw Kedron's horse. They attacked it and had another meal to last for a few more days.

Boren and Kedron were escaping. Boren decided to take the horse down the hill slowly. It was too treacherous to go any faster. The shale was slick and loose. They mostly slid down the hill but their horse did a good job of keeping his hooves under him. It wasn't long before they were at the bottom of that awful hill. They were making much better time now that they were on flatter land. They stopped to rest then. They drank a bit of water and let their horse drink from the stream nearby. They were entering the forest now. It was cooler and they could see the road ahead. It was still dark, so they decided to find a good place to sleep where they would be safer.

"Kedron, we escaped! Thanks to those terrible creatures. Did you see them? They had red glowing eyes like Neberon and they looked really hungry."

"I did see them and it was terrifying. But they ate Andoron! I can't believe it! It's exactly what he deserved. He was an evil man. I'm so glad we don't have to find out what he would have done to us if we made it to the cave of Neberon. And we didn't even have to do anything to him ourselves. I'm so glad it's over with him. Let's find a good sleeping place here somewhere. How about under one of the pine trees? I think we'd be pretty safe there. We could tie the horse close by. What do you think?"

"Good idea, Kedron. I see one now just over there."

So the two boys were able to spend a quiet night without the worry of Andoron and his evil plans for them. It was such a relief they could hardly believe it. They would worry about getting to Anakik later, not now that they had survived Andoron. They were once again traumatized by an evil man. It was over now, but the effects would last.

They woke up later in the day. The sun was up, but the forest remained softly growing lighter. The shade under the pine tree was cool and comforting. They finally woke up and realized they didn't have their packs with them. They were left at the shelf where Andoron was killed. Now, food was a problem. There was a stream that was still nearby, but what to eat? It was late summer, so maybe they could find some berries or something. They drank from the stream and looked around until they found a great berry bush with lots of berries on it. They ate until they were full, they found the horse and Boren helped Kedron get up. They rode faster this time. The road was clearly marked and dry. It was a beautiful day of sunshine and fresh air.

They made good time now that they knew where they were going. They didn't need the trail that Andoron had taken. So, they stayed on the main road and stopped when they were tired and hungry. Their horse was so good. He was stronger than he looked and since they stopped often to rest, he was able to keep going too.

When it started getting late, they found another pine tree to sleep under. They also found some mushrooms to eat and wild onions. There was a larger creek not far from the road. They decided to try their luck at fishing. Kedron suggested they try to scoop one out of the water onto the dry land. They would kill it and maybe eat it raw. That didn't sound very appetizing, but they were really getting hungry by now. Boren was able to get a fish out of the water. Kedron hit it with a rock. It turned out that raw fish wasn't too bad after all. So they cut it in half with a sharp rock and ate it. They were learning some important survival skills. They were able to sleep well that night. Their stomachs were really full for once. It felt so good.

The next morning, they decided to try fishing again. Kedron got one this time. It was bigger and harder to kill. But Boren finally got the job done. They used the same sharp rock from the day before to share it. It was pretty good and they were full again. They found some berries and ate them for dessert. Life was good now.

Kedron finally spoke, "Boren, we've been really lucky so far. Escaping Andoron was something I didn't think we could ever do. Look at us now. We're free again and our horse is strong and able to carry both of us. We've figured out how to get food here in the forest. Even though things are pretty good right now, I really wish we were back with Roslin and Karmine and our friends, Mika and Lorin. Don't you?"

"I do miss them. It's good to know we can take care of ourselves if we have to. But I'm really getting tired of it. Roslin's cooking is so much better than our raw fish, right?"

Kedron laughed and said, "Yes, for sure."

There had been plenty of grass for their horse to eat and the creek was fresh and good. Boren helped Kedron back on the horse again and they were on their way once more. This was their third day traveling. Now there were a few villagers traveling to and from the local villages. Kedron wanted to stop in one and find out if they could get some real food from a kind person. They rode slowly through one of the villages. It was called Kinsing. The villagers saw the two small boys traveling alone and asked if they needed some food. There was a café in the village and one of the couples that lived there took them to the café and fed them a warm meal of soup and bread with some fresh milk. It was so good that the boys both ate it all and asked for more. The owner was happy to give them another bowl of soup and some more bread.

Boren and Kedron were so grateful they got tears in their eyes. The villagers saw their tears and hugged them and sent them on their way. Boren had told them of their need to get to Solvig. So, they rode out of the village and continued on their way. Having the soup and bread was so good. It had been a while since they had eaten anything so nice.

Their horse seemed to know where they were going now. He moved forward without guidance and headed straight for Solvig. They were getting close now. They began to recognize places they had stopped on their way when they were running from Zedoc, the evil farmer that had kept them so long. They were going faster now that they knew they were getting close.

They rounded a corner of the road and literally ran into Karmine and some of his friends looking for them. They were a few day's journey to Solvig by then. It was a happy reunion for sure. Karmine jumped off his horse and pulled Kedron from the horse and then Boren and hugged them both as though his life depended on it.

"I can't believe we found you already! What happened to you? Where's Andoron? Are you alright? We've missed you terribly. We finally checked with the people in Anakik and they told us that you never made it there. We were worried sick. So I got my friends here to come with me to find you both. We couldn't have lived with it if you had been hurt."

Karmine's friends were happy to see them too. They remembered them riding into Solvig alone and dirty with sad tales to tell. Now they gathered around to hear the boys tell their story. That's when Karmine realized they needed to be someplace comfortable for all that. So they got back on their horses with Karmine helping the boys get back up. They all rode to the nearest village for some food and talking. Boren and Kedron had just eaten, but they were up for more food to be sure. It took them about an hour to get to the next village, so they were actually hungry again.

There was a small village nearby with a café near the center of town. They all went inside to get a meal. When they were all settled in at the cafe to eat, Boren started the tale of what had happened to them since they left Solvig with Andoron. When he told them about Andoron taking them away from Anakik, the men were angry. Then when he told them about how Andoron was treating them, they were angrier still.

Kedron got to tell the rest of it. He told them about the hill with the loose shale and the shelf they finally found to sleep on. The men were getting even angrier that Andoron would be so uncaring. When Kedron told them about the creatures and how scary they were, the men cringed. When he told them that those same creatures had eaten Andoron, and that's how they got away, they burst into hysterical laughter.

Karmine said through tears of laughter, "Well, isn't that nice? A fitting end to a no good man." It was generally agreed by all. The realization of what the boys had just endured sobered them up. "You poor kids. We're so glad you survived all that nastiness. You've been through too much for such young boys. We'll keep you safe from now on. No more trips with people we don't really know."

Karmine was especially sorrowful. It was he and Roslin who thought Andoron was a good man and would take the boys straight to Anakik. To find out that he was not what they thought he was, was too much for Karmine. He had tears in his eyes thinking about it. He felt so bad that he apologized to the boys.

"I'm so sorry, boys. Letting you go with Andoron was my fault. I should have suspected him, but he was so good at pretending to be nice, that I fell for it. It almost cost you your lives. I could not have stood it if it had. You two mean the world to Roslin and me."

"You couldn't have known, although Kedron had a pretty good idea. I should have listened to him when he wanted to go back. So, it's not all your fault. I need to listen to Kedron when he has those feelings. I'm sorry, Kedron, for not listening to you."

Kedron replied, "I'm really glad you're learning to listen to me. It would have saved us a lot of trouble, you know."

"I know, and I promise to do better."

After eating a meal of bacon, eggs, and potatoes, with more milk to drink, they headed for Solvig. Karmine helped the boys onto their horse and they were off. They were in a bigger hurry now. Karmine knew Roslin was worried and would be so happy to see the boys again. But she would also be sad about their experiences with Andoron.

They spent one night in another village at an inn there. They had dinner of roast chicken and potatoes. They were happy and getting sleepy too. Everyone had a room and the boys had their own room. It was so wonderful they couldn't believe it. They got to sleep in a bed for the first time in more than a week. It felt great! Karmine had the room next door with a passageway between so that if the boys needed him, he was close by. He didn't want to take any chances with them again.

In the morning, they had breakfast and washed up a bit before heading out of the village for Solvig. It wasn't far to go now. They would all be back there in four more days. All of the men were protective of the boys. They could see that they had been traumatized from their experience and needed reassurance that they would be safe.

Kedron was finally feeling at ease with these men who cared for them like no one had before except for Roslin and Karmine. His sense of danger had passed and he knew these men were what they seemed to be, really good men. Boren could sense Kedron relaxing, so he could too. What a difference a day could make. They had been on the verge of despair and now they felt safe and cared for. Life could be tricky sometimes, from one moment to the next, it was almost like anything could happen. For now, he was grateful for the time with Karmine and his friends.

CHAPTER 24

KARMINE AND HIS FRIENDS

KARMINE AND HIS six friends kept Boren and Kedron in the middle of their group as they traveled back to Solvig. They were in full protection mode now. There were many more people on the road and it was probably true that some of them were not good people. The men would take no chances with the boy's safety and kept an eye on those who seemed suspicious.

At midday, they stopped in a village by the name of Obinville that had an inn. They were serving the midday meal as the men entered. There was a large table near the back of the inn that they headed for. There was plenty of room for everyone. Boren and Kedron were placed near the rear of the table close to the wall to protect them. All was going very well.

The innkeeper suggested the special which was roast beef, fried potatoes, and crusty bread with ale or water to drink. It was agreed that they would have that for all of them. The boys were in agreement too. It sounded really good.

Since the boys had their back to the wall, they could see anyone coming in the door of the inn. The food came and they all ate heartily. The meal was great. When they were almost finished eating, a small group of men came in that made Kedron nervous. He nudged Boren and told him to look at the group. They appeared to be like everyone else, but Kedron sensed something off about them. They wore mostly leather pants and hats. Their shirts were a dirty gray and their faces were hard and sly-looking. The tallest of them looked the meanest and he had a scar on his left cheek that made him even scarier. He seemed to be the leader. It was apparent to Kedron that these men meant trouble, especially the tall man. He kept looking at Boren and half smiled, showing his brown teeth.

Karmine was sitting next to Boren and wondered what was going on. He looked over at Kedron and said, "Kedron, what's happening? Do you sense something about these men that we should know about?"

Kedron was becoming more and more nervous as he watched those men. The tallest of them had noticed the boys and alerted his companions that they were there. Karmine looked up and saw them. He nodded to his friends that there might be danger coming their way. They all touched their weapons and made ready to draw them if needed. They were armed with knives and short swords to protect the boys. They had recently heard news of a gang of men who were involved in kidnapping children and using them for sex slaves and selling them for their organs. Could this group of men be that gang or one like it?

This new group of men walked toward their table. The tallest of the men, the obvious leader, came near them and said, "I see all you men have a couple of good-looking boys with you. Are you having fun with them? We have money and would like to purchase them from you. We have many people who would be interested in taking them off your hands. Surely, two boys are a nuisance to you. We would relieve you of them for any price you might ask." He said the last with a nasty smirk.

As a group, the men at the table rose from their chairs with knives and short swords drawn. The group of men that approached them drew their own knives. Their leader put up his hands and said, "Wait a minute everyone, we come in peace and just wanted to make you an offer. We're hungry for young boys right now and only meant to get them from you in an easy way. But since you've decided to make it difficult, we will oblige." He snarled.

He backed away and let his men attack Karmine's group. People in the inn left in a panic running out the door. The innkeeper by the name of Rosko, ducked behind the bar and prayed he would survive. Karmine sent the boys under the table to protect them. They stayed close to the wall.

The fighting started when one of the other men tried to attack Karmine's friend, Max. Max was able to dispatch this man with ease. He was very good with his knife and knocked the other man's knife out of his hand and cut his throat. He lay dying on the floor. His mates were shocked that one of their own could be eliminated so easily. It was then that their leader realized these men were prepared and would do his group great harm if they kept going. He wasn't willing to give up even so. The boys would bring them a lot of money if they could just get them away from this group.

Soon knives were swinging and men were falling dead from knife wounds. There was much blood on the floor making the footing very tricky. Men were sliding around trying to fight each other. Karmine went after the leader of the group. The others stopped fighting to watch them. Karmine had kept it secret that he was an expert swordsman. In his youth, he had been in the military for a few years and earned awards for his skills as a swordsman. Roslin didn't suspect such a thing. She met him after he got out of the military.

So, Karmine was prepared to destroy this evil man. He used all his training to fight him. It was the fight of his life even so. Karmine was wounded once, but he had wounded the other man several times, but no killing blows. He was playing with the man to wear him out so he could eliminate him when he was getting slow. Finally, the man left an opening and Karmine stabbed him in the heart. The man fell with the look of disbelief on his face. When their leader fell, the other men ran out the door and were gone.

Karmine fell to the floor and clutched his side where he had been wounded. His friends helped him up and checked his wound. It was pretty bad and was bleeding too much. The innkeeper had some skill with bandaging the wounded. He had also served in the military and was a medic. The Wolf Wars had brought many good men into the military to protect their country and their families from a pack of wolves led by a witch by the name of Zora.

Rosko had bandages and brought them to Karmine. He was able to clean the wound and realized it was too deep to bandage. He told Karmine that he would need to get his needle and sew him up. Karmine was not happy about that and told him so. Rosko ignored his protests and went and got his needle and some gut he used for the purpose. Rosko gave Karmine a glass of hard liquor to numb him up a bit and a leather strap to bite and started sewing. Karmine tried his best not to scream and succeeded pretty well. But he chewed the leather strap he was given nearly in two.

After the stitching was done, Rosko wrapped bandages around his chest. They were tight enough to stop the bleeding, but not so tight as to restrict his breathing. The wound was quite long and deep. It was a wonder that Karmine had been able to keep fighting with such a wound. Karmine loved the boys and would never let anyone hurt them if he had to die to prevent it.

The boys were remembered and brought out from under the table. They were both terrified, and huddled together in fear. They saw Karmine was wounded and ran to him. They hugged him and cried. Karmine reassured them that he was going to be fine. He just needed some rest. Kedron and Boren were so relieved that they cried even more.

The others were checked for wounds and whether they needed any care. None of Karmine's friends were killed, but a couple of them were wounded enough to require bandaging. It wasn't terribly serious. The other friends were able to take care of them with the use of Rosko's bandages. There were four of the cartel's men that had been killed so it was necessary to let the town mortician take care of burying them. He would have help to do so.

Karmine was taken care of and was doing alright. He had lost a bit of blood, but not enough to be life threatening. It was a good thing that Rosko was there with his needle and bandages so soon after the fight was over. Karmine would need some rest, so his friends asked Rosko if he had enough rooms for all of them to stay a couple of nights with Karmine.

Rosko told them he did have several open rooms they were welcome to use. He told them not to worry about paying and just stay as long as needed. Karmine thanked him and they were led to the rooms available for them. Karmine was hoping they would only need one night for him to rest. He was weak now, but he was pretty sure he would heal quickly. Boren and Kedron wanted to stay with Karmine in case he needed something in the night. Karmine agreed and there were a couple of cots brought in so they could sleep in the same room. Kedron felt safer in the same room as his new hero.

Karmine was resting, and in the morning, he was a little stiff and sore besides the aching of his wound. When breakfast was called, he tried to get up, but fell back on the bed. He was too sore and weak to move that far. Boren told him they would bring him some food.

Everyone was in the dining area eating breakfast when they arrived. Karmine's friends started asking them about Karmine and how he was feeling. They were concerned that he hadn't come to breakfast.

Boren said, "Karmine is feeling weak this morning and wants to rest. Kedron and I will bring him his breakfast. Mr. Rosko, would you please make Karmine a plate so he can have breakfast too?"

Rosko replied, "Of course, he saved my inn with his great friends. I have a plate ready for him and two for you as soon as you come back."

"Thanks, Mr. Rosko!" Boren and Kedron followed him to the kitchen to get Karmine's plate. Boren took it to their room and gave him his food. Kedron brought his ale.

Karmine was touched and thanked the boys for helping him. The boys were embarrassed, they were proud to help him. He was their hero. Karmine sent them to the kitchen to eat their own breakfast. So, they reluctantly left him and went to eat.

Rosko had their plates ready in the kitchen and brought it to them when they entered the dining room. They were hungry and enjoyed the flapjacks and eggs on their plates. It was so good. Karmine's friends wanted to know if they could go visit Karmine now. Boren told them they were welcome to go talk with Karmine. He was probably finishing his breakfast by now.

Boren and Kedron kept eating and wanted a little more. So Rosko brought them more eggs and flapjacks. The boys continued to eat heartily until they could hold no more. They were moaning from eating too much when they finally walked away and back to their room. Rosko laughed softly at them and loved that they were so happy with his breakfast that they would eat so much.

The boys got to their room just as Karmine was saying, "I'm really worried about my wound. It hurts too much and I'm not healing very fast. I thought I could get around a bit today, but I can't. I'm afraid I'll need a bit more time before I can even get on a horse. If any of you need to leave, go ahead. I'll be back to Solvig as soon as I can."

Two of the men had to leave for family reasons, but the other four stayed to help Karmine as much as he needed. The boys walked in and ran to Karmine. "Oh, Karmine, we'll stay with you too. We can't leave you now. You're our hero."

Karmine smiled. He loved these two boys so much and was so grateful for their concern. He was also grateful that they wanted to stay. His friends would help him keep them safe here. They would hopefully be back in Solvig in a couple of days. The trouble was, his wound was much deeper than he realized. Even though Rosko had to use stitches to close the wound, Karmine still wouldn't believe he'd been injured seriously. He would learn soon enough that deep wounds like his do not heal just because one doesn't believe they are bad.

CHAPTER 25

KARMINE HEALS

AFTER TWO MORE days of Karmine needing rest and healing, two more of his friends left. Their families really did need them. What Karmine didn't know was that the other friends who left first had told Roslin all about what had happened and that Karmine would likely not be coming home for a while.

Of course, Roslin decided she needed to be with her husband and care for him. So, she took their two boys and the wagon with what they would need as they traveled and headed for the town of Obinville to be with Karmine, Boren, and Kedron.

Roslin finally arrived in Obinville two days later. She had stayed at an inn in a small town on the way. When she walked into the inn where Karmine was resting, she asked where he was. Rosko was more than happy to tell her.

She nearly ran to his room, with her boys right behind. They came into his room and ran up to Karmine and hugged him and kissed him before he could even speak. Boren and Kedron jumped up from their bed and ran to their friends. They were so glad to see them again.

Karmine was shocked and happy at the same time. He was so glad to see Roslin and the boys. He got tears in his eyes that they were really there with him. He had been trying to get healed so he could get home to them, but now they were here.

"Ah, my love, it is the sweetest thing that's happened to me in a long time that you would come and see me here. I've missed my family terribly."

"I would hope so, my darling. We finally heard what had happened to you and the boys and I decided we needed to be here with you. It's been lonely without you and Boren and Kedron around. I must hear what happened to you all while you've been gone."

"I heard that Andoron was not what he appeared to be in the village. He was really evil, wasn't he? Can you tell me what happened, Boren? I heard bits from Karmine's friends. But I don't think they knew the half of it."

Boren thought for a minute, then said, "Kedron knew something before I did. It took me a little more time to see the real Andoron. He had tools he was going to use on us. He was also planning on experimenting with magic on us. He said he wanted to be like Neberon. We were really scared."

"But how did you get away? He was big and strong."

Kedron decided to tell that part of the story, "He was so mean and wouldn't let us rest. We were really hating him. Then when we were almost to the cave where Neberon used to live, we found a shelf with an overhang on this hill we were trying to climb. It was too steep to go on and we were really tired. So we decided to sleep on the shelf away from all the shale on that hill. It was really quiet.

"Then suddenly, there were these skinny, scary creatures with big round eyes that shown red in the night. They attacked Andoron right away. So we sneaked toward our horse and I finally got on with Boren's help. We had to hurry because the creatures were eating Andoron and we didn't want to wait around until they got to eating us."

"Oh, Kedron, you and Boren have surely been through it, haven't you? How did you find your way back down here?"

Boren spoke up, "All we knew was that we needed to get down from those hills. The shale was tricky. Our horse was a wonder. He got down there really fast. I think he knew that those creatures might eat him too. We did hear Andoron's horse scream once on the way down. We kept riding 'til we thought maybe we were safe. Then we stopped and rested a couple of times. We ate raw fish and berries. Then just when we had given up on being helped, Karmine and his friends came around the corner of the road and found us. We were so happy to see them, I can tell you. So we went with them to the next village and found this inn to stay in. We had real food and slept in a real bed for the first time since we left your house."

"Then you were there when those terrible men came in and wanted to buy you, right?"

Karmine said, "It was really terrible alright. The thing is, I think we've talked about horrible things long enough. How about some food and talking about other things?"

"That makes sense, my dear. It smelled like dinner was being prepared when we came in." She sent her boys to check on the kitchen and hurry back.

A moment later, Mika ran into the room, "Mom! Dinner's ready! We're starving! Hurry! Rosko is serving right now."

Roslin agreed and told Karmine she would bring him some food.

Boren and Kedron followed them to the dining area where Rosko was serving roast pork with potatoes and vegetables. He had also baked some sourdough bread. Roslin took a plate up to Karmine and one for herself. They ate their dinner together and left the boys to eat what they wanted in the dining area. The boys ate plenty, it was really good. When they had their fill, they went back to Karmine's room to visit with Roslin. She was so nice and they knew she loved them.

Roslin told Karmine all that had happened after he left to find Boren and Kedron. She told them of problems with the pigs and the neighbor's dog. Everyone laughed at her stories. They were really funny and took their minds off the problems they've had. Karmine didn't laugh too much because his wound hurt him when he did. He really was healing, just not as fast as he thought he should. He could just about get out of bed and walk around the room now. He was hoping that in the morning he would be able to walk to breakfast. He would likely need help, but at least he might be able to get out of his room for a short while. He was beginning to hate the color of the walls. They were a nauseating yellow.

Karmine said, "Maybe we could get a separate room for the four boys that's connected to this one. Roslin, would you mind that?"

"Mind it? I would love it. I'll go talk to Rosko right now."

So she went out of the room to find Rosko. He was in the kitchen dishing up dessert. It was peach cobbler. Roslin was happy to find him doing something fun. So, when he was finished, she said, "Rosko, would it be possible for us to have a room connected to Karmine's for the boys?"

Rosko got a gleam in his eye and said, "I sure do. You can have that for the boys at no charge. I'm so grateful for Karmine. He saved the inn and me from those horrible men. He's my hero now."

Roslin was touched. Karmine was really such a good man. She said, "Thank you, Rosko. I feel the same way about him. He's been my hero forever."

She was excited to tell Karmine and the boys about their room next to Karmine's. The boys were excited too. They would have fun sleeping in the same room together. So everyone was happy.

They went to their room and found two large beds. They also had a table they could use for games and drawings. It was perfect.

CHAPTER 26

PROBLEMS TO SOLVE

G RETA WAS REALLY concerned about Zarcon. He wasn't eating enough to survive. He would drink some water and get out of bed long enough to take a short walk in the village to see how the villagers were doing. He loved being a part of the village life, if only for a few minutes. Greta always went with him and supported him as he was walking. They were often seen together in the afternoons greeting the villagers and enjoying the sunshine.

One sunny day, they were walking as usual when Zarcon suddenly fell to the ground and couldn't get up. Greta called for help. One of the villagers ran to get Magg and Matton to help. They got there quickly and helped Zarcon to his feet. He was very shaky and was unable to walk on his own. Matton was on one side with Magg on the other.

Magg asked, "What happened, Greta? What's going on with Zarcon?"

"He's not been eating much lately and I think he got so weak that today it all caught up with him. He was walking fine yesterday, but he was really tired when I got him back to his bed. I should have known then that a walk today might not be a good idea. But he loves his walks and I couldn't deny him."

Zarcon spoke up then, "Alright, I admit I haven't had any appetite lately. But I thought I was eating enough to go for short walks through the village. But today, I was doing pretty well until I wasn't. I think I passed out for a second or two and that's why I fell. I'm sorry you had to come and rescue me."

"Zarcon, you are more important than you realize. You must ask for help any time you think you might need it. Your fall was too scary for the rest of us.

"Let's get you into bed for a long rest. Let's see if you can eat more and get your strength built back up."

"Magg, you know I'm dying. There is no building anything back up at this point. Neberon has killed me and I am tired of fighting it. I'm so sick. I really feel the need to get out among the villagers and get some sunshine. I want to do that with whatever help I'll need. Are you willing to help me do that?"

"Oh, Zarcon, we will be glad to help you do that. We'll figure out what that means as time goes by. I'm sorry this is so hard for you. We have counted on you for so much. Now it's your turn to count on us. Please let us know anytime you need anything. We're ready to help in any way we can. Greta will keep us informed and we'll visit more often. Greta, please let us know when you need help, alright?"

"I have tried to do everything myself and now I see that we both need your help. I want Zarcon to be happy and have all that he needs at this time. I will do better at keeping you informed when we need your help."

"We love you both. We will check back with you later today, unless you need us sooner."

Magg and Matton decided it would be a good idea to let Jarrone and his family know what was going on with Zarcon. So, they headed for his family cottage on the edge of the village. They knocked on the door of the cottage to talk with the family.

Jarrone came to the door, "Hello, what's going on? Come in and let's talk."

Magg and Matton smiled at Jarrone and were happy to see him. His family came into the room to see what was going on.

"Hi, Magg! It's so good to see you again," said Lucintha.

"It's good to see you, too, Lucintha. We came to talk to all of you about what's going on in the village and Zarcon in particular. Jarrone, do you remember that he was hit by one of Neberon's flying glass shards?"

"I do. How is Zarcon doing now?"

"That's what I came to talk to you about. He's not doing well right now. We've tried everything we know of to help him, but nothing is working. He is failing fast right now. I have healing magic, but this thing is too strong and is taking over Zarcon's body. I'm not sure how much longer he will last."

"Oh no! We can't lose Zarcon. Would it be a bad thing if I try to see what I can do? I know you have much stronger magic, but maybe with the help of my mother's book, I can find another way to help him."

"Jarrone, I'm so sorry I didn't think of you before. I know you have stronger magic than you even think. Will you come with us now to try to help him?"

"I would be honored. Let's go now!"

The three of them headed back to Zarcon's room to see if Jarrone could help him. It seemed like a possibility. There was a bit of excitement at the thought that maybe Jarrone could do something that Magg could not.

They entered the inn and knocked on Zarcon's door. Greta answered and let them in.

"I'm so glad you came. Zarcon is having a tough day of it today. Ever since he fell, he's felt ill. I'm really worried about him. Will you check him over, Magg?"

"Greta, I brought Jarrone because maybe he can do something I can't. He has very strong magic and with his mother's Book of Magic, maybe he'll find another way to help. Are you alright with Jarrone checking him over instead?"

"Of course, Magg. Jarrone, I'm so glad to see you. I do hope you can think of a way to help Zarcon. We've tried everything we know how to do."

Jarrone stepped forward and looked at Zarcon. "Is it alright if I check you over and see if there's anything I can do to help?"

"You can, Jarrone, but I'm feeling like it might be a bit too late. But do whatever you think will help."

Jarrone looked into Zarcon's body and saw the damage the poison had done to him. He was discouraged by what he saw, but kept looking for a possible solution to the situation. As he examined the poison, he found a place where it was weak. It was really difficult to spot, but it was there.

Jarrone started to smile just a bit when he realized he could indeed help Zarcon. He began a chant that was complicated and musical. He had memorized it long ago when his mother told him about its curative power. He was really excited to get to finally use it on someone he really cared about.

The longer he chanted, the greater effect it seemed to be having on Zarcon. He had kept his eyes closed and was worried that this wouldn't work either. Slowly, he opened his eyes and had a look of shock on his face. He was actually feeling better. How could this be? He was so sure he was going to die.

"Jarrone, what are you doing to me?"

"Helping you. Now, be quiet while I work."

Jarrone kept chanting, then he began to sing a beautiful melody. It seemed to weave magic in and around Zarcon as he sang. Zarcon's body seemed to fill back out where he had grown so thin. His cheeks became almost rosy.

Jarrone finally ended the spell and asked Zarcon how he felt.

Zarcon started to laugh. "I've never felt better, my boy! I've never seen anyone bring someone back from death like this." At that, he sat up and kissed Greta soundly on the mouth and hugged her close.

"Jarrone, you are more than incredible! I didn't even know such magic was possible. You seem to have power over death. Can that be true?"

"No, I just found the cure for the poison in Zarcon's body. Once it was eliminated, I was able to heal his body completely. It is complicated and draining, but worth the effort. I'm so grateful it worked. I think I will now go home and take a nap."

Magg and Matton laughed at that. "I know just how you feel, dear boy. But I think it would be better if you took your nap here in the inn. You're much too exhausted to walk home."

"You're right, of course. Where's the nearest bed?"

"This way, Jarrone."

Jarrone followed Magg to the nearest empty room and fell on the bed, instantly falling asleep. Matton met her outside the room door.

"Wow! Jarrone did what I just saw and I still don't believe it! What power!"

Meanwhile, Greta and Zarcon continued holding each other and laughing. It was too good to be true that Zarcon was better than ever.

Magg sent Matton to get Jasmine and Donavan to come to Zarcon's room. They needed to know what had happened with Zarcon. Matton found them walking in the forest near the waterfall where he and Magg liked to go.

"Jasmine, Donavan, come quick, Jarrone just did the impossible. Come and see for yourselves."

"We'll come with you right now. This is incredible!" Jasmine said. Both of them hurried to follow Matton to Zarcon's room. They were practically running when they got there. It was plain to see that Zarcon was doing very well.

"Zarcon, what happened to you? We just heard that you've been treated by Jarrone with his magic," Donavan said.

Zarcon saw Donavan and Jasmine. "I'm so glad you've come. I'm feeling perfectly well. I know it sounds odd. I don't know why I was healed. It's like a miracle. I know Terrence has been gone for two years now and I've lost my dog, Voltar, as well. It's been hard for me to lose them both. I was assuming it was my turn. My life has been good. I was able to help eliminate Neberon and that makes me happy. I'm so glad that I have lived long enough to see him gone for good."

"We worked hard to get rid of the Blue Orb before the witches could do anything harmful with it. The mist monsters were another challenge we took care of in this very village. It took all of us to do it, but we did it."

"Ah, the memories, and now I get to make more memories with the one person I am so grateful for, Greta. She is my soul mate. Now of all times, I'm thinking I want to marry her."

"Greta, come to me closer." She did so with joy in her eyes. "I've been an old fool. I thought our friendship was all we needed. But now I see that the love we share was something more than friendship. We never spoke of it, but I knew I loved you from the first day I met you. I was just too proud to think I could get married and needed marriage to make me a whole person. You've sustained me when I would have given up. You've comforted me when things were tough. I have needed you like no other. When you nearly died, I thought I would die with you. I couldn't conceive of living without your sweet spirit in my life. Please don't hate me for being such a fool all these years. Now, I will make up for it. Greta, will you marry me? I know I'm old and just escaped death, but I realize how much I need to have you as my wife for the rest of whatever life we may have together."

Greta was crying for love of Zarcon. "Zarcon, I have spent my life with you. I have loved you more each passing day. I will marry you. I found just being with you and helping you when I was needed was very rewarding to me. You've taught me much about life and magic. I do love you with all my heart." She hugged and kissed him.

The others were crying tears of joy to think that now Zarcon and Greta would finally be man and wife. So much joy where for the past few days was only grief thinking that Zarcon would die. Jarrone was truly the hero. He would find out all about it when he finally had the strength to wake up.

When Jarrone had recovered from the use of so much magic to heal Zarcon, he finally entered Zarcon's room to see what was happening. As he walked into the room, he was greeted by his friends calling him a hero and making a big fuss over him. He was embarrassed, but loved every minute of it. He felt that he had finally found out what his magic could do to help others. Healing Zarcon had taken a lot of study to figure out what was needed to heal him from the organism that was attacking him.

When Jarrone finally figured it out, he was so excited! He had sent his power into Zarcon and immediately, the spell worked! Now, he knew he could do such hard things and he was proud of himself.

Magg came close to him and told him about Zarcon and Greta's marriage to begin very soon. He was even more excited about that.

Later, Magg spoke to Jasmine about having a party for Jarrone and Zarcon and Greta.

Jasmine said, "That's a great idea! Maybe we could have dinner with our friends and give Greta her new dress. If we keep it a bit small, then when the wedding comes along, we can make it a big affair. What do you think, Magg?"

"I like that idea. A party would be the thing. We can dress up a bit and give Greta her dress to wear. It will be really nice. I think Zarcon would love it too."

"Let's talk to Aribon about the dinner and what we need to do to make it special."

They spoke to Aribon, who was happy to cook something special and make a dessert worthy of a party. It was coming together.

Later, Magg and Jasmine went to talk with Revinia about Greta's dress.

Magg smiled at Revinia and asked her if she had finished Greta's dress.

"I have, as a matter of fact. I was hoping you'd ask for it soon. Come to my room and I'll show it to you."

Revinia led them to her room at the back of the house where she kept her cloth and sewing materials. She had the dress in a box by her bed. She lifted the lid and brought out the dress for Magg and Jasmine to see.

"Oh, Revinia, it's such a beautiful dress. I know Greta will be so pleased. I'm sure Zarcon will love it too. We would like to pay you now. Also, would you like to present it to Greta tonight? We're having a party to celebrate Zarcon and Greta's engagement and Jarrone's healing of Zarcon. Will you and your family come so we can present Greta with this beautiful dress and celebrate with us?"

"I'm sure we would all love that. Thank you so much for the money. It will help me buy more fabric for more dresses. I can't wait to give it to Greta."

Magg and Jasmine walked back to the inn so happy about the dress Revinia had made for Greta. It would be even more special because of it. As they got back to the inn, they talked to Donavan and Matton about their plans for the evening. Both men agreed that it would be a wonderful evening for them all.

Jasmine and Donavan went to Zarcon's room to tell Greta about the party, "Would both of you come?"

"How exciting! It's just what we need after all this worry and concern for Zarcon. What do you think Zarcon, does it sound fun for you?"

"I think it will be wonderful!"

Jasmine said, "Then it's settled. Be ready by dinner time and we'll all celebrate."

Jasmine and Donavan went back to the dinning room to tell the others that Zarcon was coming with Greta. Now the party was complete with all their friends coming, too.

Aribon was happily cooking the dinner and planning what he would make for dessert. Alfias was there helping him get things together. Alfias was excited to see Lucintha again and join the party. Aribon told him that he could join the party and help clean up later.

~

It was almost time for the party to start. Magg and Jasmine were waiting for Revinia to come with the new dress. She came to the inn a bit early so they could show Greta the dress and help her put it on. They knocked on Zarcon's door and Greta opened to them. She was surprised to see all three of them at her door.

Revinia laid the package on the table for Greta.

As Greta opened the packaging, she gasped, "This is too beautiful for me to wear! I've never had a dress so pretty in my whole life! Revinia! You made it for me, didn't you? I love it! The color is perfect and I love the lace around the collar. I will wear it tonight and be the proudest old lady there."

As Greta put on the dress with Revinia's help, it fit her perfectly. She looked like a completely different person. She was suddenly her beautiful young self. The really happy part was that Zarcon was going to see her in it. Greta wanted to run to him right then to show him.

He was in the next room resting. She excused herself and went to show Zarcon what Revinia had made for her. He got up from his chair with tears in his eyes. She looked so lovely. He held her tight and said, "Greta, you look so beautiful! Did Revinia make this dress for you? It's stunning on you, my dear. I love you, Greta."

Magg, Jasmine, and Revinia left the room then to get themselves ready for the party. They also hugged Revinia for her hard work and kindness to Greta. She had outdone herself. It was a very happy moment for the three women.

Once everyone was ready for the party, they met in the dining room for dinner. Greta and Zarcon came in last so everyone could see them together and how lovely Greta was in her new dress. There were a lot of ohhs and ahhs when she walked in on Zarcon's arm. Then applause broke out and everyone clapped for them.

Zarcon and Greta were given seats at the head of the table in front. It was a small group of dear friends gathered together to celebrate Zarcon's healing, Jarrone's magic, and the engagement of Zarcon and Greta. Such a happy time for the friends.

Dinner was wonderful, as usual. Aribon had made roast pork, potatoes from his garden, squash, carrots, and beans on the side. When everyone had eaten their fill, Aribon brought out his dessert creation.

It was a kind of custard with caramel sauce poured over it. It was so good that it was gone in a matter of minutes. Everyone was too busy loving it to say anything until it really was gone. Aribon was praised and applauded for his efforts at making such a great dessert. He was becoming a professional at it.

As the evening wound down, the friends gathered around Jarrone and the two soon-to-be married. There were congratulations for them and hugs all around. As the guests were leaving, Alfias found Lucintha and they spent time getting to know each other better. Jarrone's father found the widow lady, Marion, and they spent time together outside in front of the inn. It was a wonderful night with a slight breeze and warm enough to sit on the chairs set on the porch. It seemed that love was in the air that night.

Indeed, Zarcon and Greta left the party early arm in arm. Time alone was a priority now that both of them were well and even more in love. The events of the recent past had made them both more appreciative for their health and time together. Once in the room they shared, Zarcon helped Greta out of her new dress. They both were grateful to spend time in bed together where they could spend the night holding each other close.

CHAPTER 27

KARMINE CONTINUES TO HEAL

THE NEXT MORNING, Karmine was finally feeling good enough to walk to the dining room for breakfast. He made it all the way with the help of Roslin. He was able to sit at the table and eat. The boys were happy to see him able to move around a bit. He was getting better faster now. Roslin and Karmine were also thinking he might be able to travel soon.

Breakfast was really good. They had fried potatoes, bacon, eggs, and pancakes. The boys were eating all they could get down. Karmine ate better than he had in a week. Roslin was glad to see that. She was able to eat quite a lot herself.

There were a few other guests at breakfast chatting among themselves. It was a pleasant meal. It was also a sunny day. It had been raining at night for a few days. The air was crisp and clean and smelled wonderful. The rain had settled the dust on the road, too.

After the boys and Roslin and Karmine had all they wanted to eat, they went back to their rooms so Karmine could rest. The short walk to the dining area had worn him out. Roslin was a bit worried about that. The boys went to their room and played together. They made tents out of their blankets and had a great time.

Roslin needed to talk with Karmine. She was concerned about getting back home to Solvig. "Karmine, I know you're getting better, I just feel like we need to get back to Solvig as soon as we may. Do you have any idea how many more days you'll need before we can go back?"

"I'm feeling better and my wound doesn't hurt nearly like it did, even yesterday. I think that's why I can walk to the dining area. If this keeps up, I'll be able to try riding a horse maybe the day after tomorrow. How does that sound?"

"It sounds good, my dear. I will help you every way I can to help you heal and move forward. I love you, you know."

"I love you too. You are my heart."

They kissed and soon were making gentle love to each other. It was just what they needed.

Later on, they went back to the dining area for dinner. Again, Karmine was able to walk. Roslin helped him get settled at the table. The boys were happy to be eating again. They chased each other around the table for a minute then settled down when they got that look from Roslin. Boren and Kedron were happier than they could remember being.

Kedron's two friends that had stayed were still there. They had kept to themselves because Roslin was there to help Karmine. Max and Teo were the friends that stayed. They were there in case of any sign of trouble until they could get back to Solvig. They were really good friends to Karmine. Roslin was very grateful for their presence. She felt safer because Karmine was not able to fight just yet.

Max and Teo were aware of anyone coming in as they ate their dinner. Since the men from the gang had come in to buy the boys, they had been hyper-alert to any of them returning. It had been very quiet since the fight. But continued quiet could not be counted on. There were many bad people on the road these days.

As they watched the door to the inn, they noticed two men looking at the inn as if trying to decide whether to go in or not. It appeared they were arguing about it. Suddenly, Max recognized one of the men to be from the fight. He had a bandage on his arm. Max knew then that he was indeed part of the gang. Max motioned to Teo what he was seeing. Teo prepared to fight. He motioned to Karmine to leave the dining area and take the boys with him. Karmine signaled to Roslin that they must go to their rooms immediately.

They gathered the boys and took them to the rooms they shared. They moved quickly and when they got to the room, they locked the door and put the dresser in front of the door. They did the same to the boy's door.

Suddenly, they heard a loud crash and fighting starting. A woman screamed as they ran out of the dining area to get away from the fighting. It was horrible for Karmine to have to hide when his friends were fighting for them. He was pacing the room and couldn't relax. Roslin finally stopped him and made him sit down on the bed.

"Karmine, you're going to wear yourself out with all that pacing and it's not helping anyone."

"You're right, Roslin. I have to take care of myself, but this is so hard on me to stay up here hiding when my friends might be dying."

"I know that Rosko will come and let us know when it's over. Either him or Max or Teo. We have to try to wait patiently if we can. The boys have to stay with us in case we must protect them. We can't take any chances of harm coming to them."

"You're right, of course. Patience is the most difficult thing for me to do. I just don't have any."

"I understand. It really is the hardest virtue to learn." She smiled at that. She knew she was not the most patient person either. But she kept working on it. She knew Karmine did too.

In the dining area, Max and Teo were fighting the two men that had come in with knives. They fought hard and were pretty good with their knives. Max and Teo were better, however. Max cut one of them on the other arm and as Teo was fighting the other man, he left an opening and Teo was able to cut him deeply in the chest.

Both men decided they would take the better part of valor and run away. They were bleeding pretty badly, but if they wanted to run away, that was their choice. They were seen mounting horses and heading out of the village at high speed.

Max had been scratched on his arm and Teo wasn't hurt at all. Rosko came to them as soon as the other two men ran away. He could see that Max was injured so he brought his medical kit to bandage his arm. Teo went to Karmine's room to tell them that the fight was over and Max had been wounded on his arm. Rosko was bandaging him even then.

Roslin and Karmine went to Max in the dining area. Rosko assured them that the wound was not bad. He did need a couple of stitches, however. Max bore it bravely and smiled when Karmine came into the room.

"Well, it looks like we both have scars from this journey. I'm so glad you're doing better, Karmine. Maybe we'll be going back in a couple of days. What do you think?"

"I'm doing my best to heal. But yes, I'm getting better finally. I'm walking better and I'm going to try getting on a horse in a couple of days."

"Good, I'll help anyway I can."

"Thank you, Max. I have such great friends. You and Teo are the best friends I've ever had."

"Well, we're here for you, Karmine. It was our honor to fight for you and the boys. We couldn't think of what would have happened if we hadn't been here. So, that's why we're here, because we love you and your family."

"I want you to know that I'm grateful and love you both."

It was getting late and Roslin helped the boys wash up and get ready for bed. They needed a bit of comforting after the experience of the night. They hadn't seen anything, but they had heard the fighting and saw Max's wound bandaged up. So Roslin stayed with them telling them happy stories until they went to sleep.

Karmine was sleeping already, he had been worn out by all the excitement, too. Roslin got ready for bed and joined him, hugging him tight as they slept.

Max and Teo were grateful to head for bed. The fighting had worn them out and they needed lots of rest. The day had been a difficult one. Max was going to be fine in a few days. He was glad for the chance to rest before they would need to get back to Solvig.

The next morning, Karmine woke early and walked around the room. He was feeling much better. Roslin woke up and watched Karmine walking. She could see that he was stronger. She was so glad to see it. She finally spoke to Karmine.

"My dear, you are doing so much better this morning. How is your wound today?"

"It's still a bit tight, but the pain is nearly gone. I'm going to try getting on a horse today. I really want to get back home."

"Are you sure? Don't do that too soon and open your wound again. Let Rosko check it to make sure it's healing enough for all that."

"Oh, alright. Let's ask him after breakfast. I want to wash up before breakfast and dress in some clean clothes."

"Sounds like a good idea. Let's check on the boys and see if they're up yet."

Roslin went to the door and opened it to find the boys still asleep. They looked so sweet. She was so grateful they were in her life. She was also grateful that they had been protected. She stood there for a few minutes then decided to let them sleep a bit longer.

Roslin was able to wash up and put on some clean clothes. She was wearing a blue dress that hugged her figure and made her look younger. She really was a pretty woman. When she was ready, she went in to wake up the boys for breakfast.

"Come on, boys, it's time to get up and go eat breakfast as soon as you're dressed."

They moaned for a moment then remembered how great breakfast was and hurried to get ready.

It wasn't long before they were all headed to the dining area to eat. Rosko had prepared a wonderful breakfast again. It was pancakes and fruit with maple syrup and scrambled eggs. He had juice to drink this morning.

Max and Teo joined them after a few minutes. Once again everyone ate all they wanted and enjoyed every bite. After eating, the boys wanted to go outside for a while. Roslin went with them to make sure they stayed safe. Max joined Roslin.

Karmine spoke with Rosko to ask him if his wound was healed well enough for him to get on a horse this day. Teo was there to help him as needed.

Rosko untied his bandage and checked the wound. "It looks pretty good, Karmine. I don't think you'll open it by getting on a horse. Just pay attention to how it feels, alright?"

Karmine agreed. He left the dining area and went to the stables to try getting on his horse. Teo brought his horse out and saddled it. He was there to help Karmine get on. Karmine put his foot into the stirrup and pulled himself up.

"Hey, Teo, it didn't hurt a bit. I think I'm ready to get back to Solvig. What do you think?"

"I think you're ready too. You got up there with the same ease as always. If it doesn't hurt at all, you're ready."

"I can't wait to tell Roslin. She'll be so pleased."

"She will."

Karmine got back down off the horse with no problem. He was pleased with himself. He and Teo walked around to the front of the inn to find Max watching Roslin and the boys playing games together. As Karmine walked up to them, Roslin went to him.

"Karmine, how did you do?"

"Roslin, I did it and it didn't hurt at all. Just ask Teo."

Teo spoke up, "He did very well, Roslin. I think he's ready to leave tomorrow."

"What great news! Karmine, I'm so happy to be able to leave this place. Too many sad memories for me and the rest of us."

"If we're leaving tomorrow, we'd better get packed up tonight. We'll leave right after breakfast in the morning."

The boys shouted, "Hooray!" It was exciting to think of going back home to Solvig. Boren and Kedron were especially excited. They loved Roslin, Karmine, and their boys. They were feeling like they were part of a family, as indeed they were.

It wasn't much longer until dinner was ready. They had played in the yard all afternoon. Roslin was truly tired when dinner was finally announced. They all ran inside to clean up for the meal. The boys were especially dirty. So, Roslin made sure they were all washed up and ready to go eat. They needed to change their dirty clothes, and with Roslin's help, they found some clean ones she had brought with her.

They headed for the dining area and sat together with Max and Teo. Karmine was able to walk without problems and sit himself down comfortably. The boys noticed and were really glad. Tomorrow would be exciting, to be back on the road home.

CHAPTER 28

HEADED HOME

THE NEXT MORNING, Karmine got up feeling even better. He was ready to get out of the inn and get on the road home. He stretched a little and his wound felt good. He was excited to get on a horse and leave. He was so glad Roslin had joined him with their boys. He was so lonely before she got there. Max and Teo had tried to keep him company, but it just wasn't the same.

Max and Teo were also glad to be getting back home. They were single and had been able to stay with Karmine. Now, they could all go home. It was such a relief.

The boys woke up early and were so excited. They had all packed their belongings the night before so all they needed to do was get dressed and eat breakfast. Their horses had been well-cared for by Rosko and his help. He had breakfast ready for when they all came to eat.

Max and Teo joined them as they went to eat. They chatted as they walked to the dining area. They were feeling happy at last. Rosko had prepared them a great breakfast again. They all ate heartily and were filled. Rosko also gave them some supplies for their ride home. He had been very generous.

Karmine said, "Rosko, you have been more than kind to us through all this. You're handiwork has helped heal my wound and I'm so grateful. We will miss you."

Rosko replied, "Well, I'm hoping you'll come back to visit once in a while. I'll miss all of you as well. It's been an adventure to me too."

Roslin added, "We will be back and bring the boys with us. You've been so kind to us, we owe you a great deal. Thank you so much."

Rosko replied, "You know, I think I owe Karmine and his friends the safety of my inn and also the safety of my guests and myself. To me, it was worth every bit of money it cost me to take care of you all. So, come back when you can and I will be more than happy to see you. Do take care out on the road. I'll pray for your safe return home."

Roslin gave Rosko a hug goodbye and climbed aboard her wagon. The boys were in the back of the wagon and Boren and Kedron were on their horse. Karmine climbed on his horse just fine and was ready to ride.

They waved at Rosko as they rode away. He waved back and was sad to see them leave. He was happy for them, especially Karmine, that he was mostly healed of his wound.

Karmine led the way up the road. Boren and Kedron rode alongside the wagon. Max and Teo followed close behind. They had food and supplies thanks to Rosko. They kept going for about three hours before they finally stopped to eat and let Karmine rest. He was doing well, but he hadn't ridden a horse for quite a while and needed to rest his legs. His wound was doing well. But he thought he should stop in another two hours for the rest of the day. He didn't want to push his luck with it.

The food Rosko sent was bread and cheese and juice and beer to drink. It was great for the road. There was plenty for all of them. They rested for an hour and then Karmine got on his horse and so did Boren and Kedron. Roslin was up in the wagon with her two sons, Mika and Lorin. Max and Teo ate with them and continued to ride close behind the wagon, and off they went back to Solvig.

They rode for another two hours. Karmine was getting tired and was ready to stop for the day. He eased off his horse and found a place to rest. Roslin was concerned. "Are you alright, dear?"

"Just a bit tired. I think I might need to ride in the wagon tomorrow. The horse is too much for now. Maybe Boren can ride my horse tomorrow. I just need a break from the horse. My wound feels alright, but I'm too tired to ride. Roslin, let Mika and Lorin ride in the back of the wagon with the supplies."

Boren said, "I'll ride your horse, Karmine. Kedron can ride our horse. He does fine."

Kedron added, "I can ride our horse alone." He said with a bit of pride.

Karmine was impressed. These two boys were much more mature for their age than he realized. Their difficult lives had matured them, sadly. Their childhood had been taken from them. He was so glad his sons were keeping it playful and more like the children they were.

They unsaddled the horses for the night and brushed them down. They let them eat the grass close to the road where Roslin left the wagon. They all ate more bread and cheese and juice. There was also fresh water to drink from a nearby brook. Max and Teo were happy to be a part of this family. They were so kind.

They chatted until it got late and found a place to sleep. They had bedrolls and used their packs for pillows. It made a comfortable night's rest. The sun came up early and shown in their faces. So, they woke up ready to eat something and move on.

Karmine said, "Looks like we're going to be home in another day and a half. We've done really well this far. I'm so grateful for all of you."

Boren said, "You've been the family we haven't had for a long time. We're the ones who are grateful. Max and Teo have been such good friends to all of us, too. But it will be great to be back home."

Boren rode Karmine's horse and Kedron rode their horse. Karmine rode in the wagon and drove it for Roslin. Mika and Lorin rode in the back of the wagon. Max and Teo were doing fine on their own horses. They rode away in the same order as before. The day went well. They stopped again after three hours and had something to eat and rest. They rested and chatted together. So far, the trip was pleasant. They only had one more day to travel and they would be back to Solvig. It was good to be so close.

They rode for another two hours and found a small inn in a very small village. They decided to spend the night there. They stayed the day and had dinner. They rented rooms for everyone and had a wonderful night in a real bed. The food had been good and filling. But they were anxious to get home. It had been too long since the boys and Karmine had been in Solvig. It was exciting to be nearly there.

CHAPTER 29

SOLVIG AT LAST

BOREN AND KEDRON were enjoying traveling with Karmine and Roslin's family and Max and Teo. They were anxious to get back to Solvig. They wanted to stay with Karmine and Roslin and their sons, Mika and Lorin. They considered themselves to be a part of the family. They felt safe with them and loved. It was a wonderful feeling.

They were getting close to Solvig and their joy was growing stronger. When the first roofs of the houses in Solvig started to show through the trees, they wanted to gallop their horses and enter the village yelling and throwing something into the air. They didn't, of course, they followed the wagon with Karmine's family in a respectable manner. As they entered Solvig, some of the villagers saw them and started yelling welcome to them. Other villagers heard them and came out of their homes to see what was going on.

All the villagers were so happy to see Karmine and Roslin with their friends, Max and Teo returning. Then they saw Boren and Kedron. They were even happier to see that they were in one piece. The whole village was cheering to see them coming. There had been so much concern in the village about the boys that now that they were doing better, they could hardly wait to talk to them about what had happened while they were away.

Karmine drove the wagon into the center of the village and stopped. Max and Teo stayed with them. Karmkine wanted to thank everyone for being supportive and welcoming them home. Roslin was so touched, she had tears in her eyes. Boren and Kedron were overwhelmed with all the excitement that they were back. Mika and Lorin were happy for the boys, but a little bit jealous. Maybe they would get a party with everyone so excited to see them come back. They could only hope.

The crowd helped Mika and Lorin down from the wagon. Boren and Kedron needed a little help getting down off their horses, too. Roslin and Karmine got down and shook the hands of so many villagers, it was kind of tiring. But they appreciated the welcoming.

One of the villagers spoke up, "Hey, now that you're all back, let's have a celebration tomorrow night! We could have lots of food and drinks and maybe games or dancing. What do you say, everyone?"

There was a cheer from everyone in favor. It was going to happen, and Mika and Lorin were satisfied to hear it, at least there would be a party. They were no longer jealous. Boren and Kedron were both delighted at the idea of a party, too. The boys were excited and decided to go play in the field near town. They asked Roslin and Karmine if it was alright if they did so before they left.

Roslin was a bit nervous to have them out of her sight so soon after getting back from their last adventure of horror. She said, "Listen, you four, I will not allow you to be out of my sight for at least a week. I'm still worried about what happened to you. Please stay near me for that week. I would really appreciate it."

The boys were disappointed, but kind of understood that it was a mother kind of thing. So they asked if they could play where they were. Roslin was happier about that and told them it was alright. Karmine was glad they went along with Roslin and didn't try to fight her over it. They were good boys after all.

Ruby, Roslin's friend, said, "Roslin, would you and the family like to have dinner at my house tonight? I've cooked plenty of food and it would be so nice to talk to you and Karmine now that you're all back home. I've missed you all so much, so has the rest of the villagers. I think you need a break from all that after what you've been through in the past few weeks. It would be great if Max and Teo came too. What do you say?"

Roslin was touched and said, "We would be honored to eat with you and your family. Thanks so much for thinking of us. I know Max and Teo would love to come. And I'll let Karmine and the boys know what we've planned. When should we come over?"

"Why don't you come in just an hour? That will give you time to change and rest a bit before dinner. I'll have dinner ready by then, too. Just finishing up a few things. See you then?"

"That sounds perfect. Thanks again, dear friend."

Roslin and Karmine gathered up the boys and they rode in the wagon back to their home. Roslin ordered everyone to clean up a bit before they were to go to dinner at Ruby's. Then they rested for a while before heading to Ruby's. Max and Teo went to their homes and cleaned up, too. It would be so nice to join Karmine and his family for dinner. Ruby was their neighbor and was a great cook.

As they arrived at Ruby's, they could smell the delicious dinner cooking. It was so great for Roslin not to have to cook after their long journey back home. They were all exhausted.

"Thank you again, Ruby. You saved the day."

Max said, "Teo and I really appreciate being invited, too. We've gotten really close to Karmine and Roslin these past couple of weeks and it's like we're part of the family."

"Well, I felt that it was the least we could do after all you have been through. Come on in and sit down at the table. The children will sit at the smaller table set aside for them. Roslin, if you can help me, we can bring the food to the table."

"I would be more than happy to help."

As they entered the kitchen, it was plain that Ruby had done a lot to make dinner for them. She had roast wild turkey, potatoes and carrots from her garden that she cooked with the turkey, and bread she had freshly baked. Ruby called Stefan, her husband, to help with the turkey. It was quite large. Ruby and Roslin carried in the rest of the meal. The children were in awe of so much food. They could hardly wait to start eating it.

Ruby asked Roslin and Karmine to tell her all about the boys and how they found them and what happened while they were gone.

"I'll let Karmine tell you how he found them and what happened at the inn one night. It's pretty scary."

Karmine started the story, "It just so happened that the boys were coming around a corner in the road not far from where we were. I was so surprised to see them coming toward us on that sorry excuse for a horse they were riding. I almost fell off my horse. I jumped down and helped them off their horse so we could talk. You know my friends were with me at the time. I'll actually let Boren and Kedron tell you about Andoron and the kind of man he turned out to be."

Boren was shy to tell them all that had happened. But he started off, "We rode away with him and were headed in the right direction at first. The thing is, Kedron had a bad feeling about him from the first day. I thought he was just being nervous, I was wrong.

"Suddenly, Andoron decided we needed to take another trail and he needed us to be with him. That's when I got scared too. He kept us moving pretty fast. We were getting really tired and Kedron could hardly keep going. Finally, we stopped and rested for a few minutes and ate something. He got weird and decided he needed to tie our hands so we couldn't escape."

"We kept moving and sleeping in the forest. Finally, we came to a tall hill we had to climb. It was shale and made climbing almost impossible. I had to get off the horse and walk us up the hill. We made it to a shelf and Aribon decided we needed to rest there for the night."

"Everything was going alright. We fell asleep. Kedron woke up and shook me. We saw some strange creatures, probably made by Neberon. They had weird red eyes that showed in the dark, like Neberon's. They attacked Andoron first. We moved slowly, crawling to our horse. We were able to get out of there before the creatures decided to attack us. We heard Andoron screaming and his horse gave one loud scream then all was quiet. Our horse made it off the hill and we camped in the forest and ate berries and raw fish until we met up with Karmine and his friends. We were never so happy to see anyone than to see Karmine coming up the road right in front of us."

Ruby and Stefan were in shock at all they had been through. But the story wasn't over yet.

"We took the boys to an inn and had dinner there. A man and ten of his gang came in and wanted to buy the boys and take them off our hands. He said they really needed them. We were so angry to hear such things that we stood up and drew our weapons. The fight was terrible. Four of the gang members were killed and I managed to kill the leader. But in the middle of the fight, he wounded me in the side. It was bad. Luckily, the innkeeper was a medic in the Wolf Wars and was able to stitch me up. I sent anyone home who needed to go and I was taken to a room to heal. It was a couple of weeks before I finally felt fit to get out bed to go to breakfast. Boren and Kedron were so good to help me, as were Teo and Max."

"Then a miracle, Roslin came to help with the boys. I was very happy and grateful to see her walk through the door of my room. I had missed her and the boys very much. I knew I was going to be just fine right then. So, I finally could get to breakfast and soon after that I could ride a horse a short distance. I kept practicing, and soon we decided to leave for home. I tried riding a horse, but got tired too soon. Boren said he would ride my horse and Kedron would ride their horse while I rode in the wagon with Roslin. Max and Teo came along behind to make sure we were all safe.

"Now, we're home and so glad to be here. It's been a difficult few weeks for all of us. But now we can heal and spend time together and relax." Boren and Kedron agreed. It felt like it had been so long since they left Solvig with Andoron.

Ruby and her family were in awe of all that had happened to them. They were so grateful that they all made it back to Solvig. They were close to tears as they listened to Karmine and the boys. He was a hero and so were the boys.

Dinner was so good and enjoyed by all. The stories sobered everyone. But at the same time, it was wonderful for them to be together again and safe, at least for now.

Ruby served her dessert of peach cobbler which was deemed "the best ever".

After dessert, it was getting late and Karmine said, "Ruby, this had been a wonderful dinner and it's so nice to be able to tell you what the last few weeks have been for us. I know for myself, I'm really worn out and need a good night's rest. We'll be heading for home now. We will see you at the party tomorrow, right? I'm looking forward to that. I know all the boys are too. So, I bid you a goodnight and a heart full of gratitude. Thank you for your kindness and wonderful food."

Max and Teo expressed their gratitude as they left. Max said, "You've been so kind to all of us, Ruby. We won't forget it."

"Karmine, it is so good to have you and your family with Max and Teo back with us. We've missed you and the boys. I'm so glad I could provide you with dinner on your first night back. We love you, you know."

Roslin hugged Ruby and thanked her, too. They left with fond goodbyes until tomorrow.

The boys were really tired too. It was good to be going home to their own beds for the night. The whole family was dragging home. They were just worn out. Roslin carried her youngest son, Lorin, while Karmine carried Mika. Boren and Kedron were able to walk because their trials had made them really strong.

It seems that in our lives trials make a person stronger and better able to cope with the daily things that come along. Not to be grateful for hard times, but in time it's easier to see what the lesson was from that trial. Boren and Kedron, young as they were, were able to see the difference in strength after so many physical challenges they had faced. They now knew they could overcome their problems together. Their bond was so much stronger now.

Life had a way of surprising a person. It was known that it was not possible to assume that things would always be the same. Fortunately, life would go on for our friends.

CHAPTER 30

A WEDDING TO PLAN

Now that the party was over, there was another wedding to plan. There had been a lot of excitement in planning Jasmine and Donavan's wedding in Synkana. Now, they could celebrate with Zarcon and Greta. They would plan the wedding and the two would be married as soon as Zarcon could be up and around and strong enough for the celebration that would follow their wedding vows. He was doing so well that it was likely only going to be a few days.

Jarrone wanted to be involved in planning the wedding. He found Magg and spoke to her about it, "Magg, I would like to be able to help with the planning, if possible. I might be able to come up with some fireworks. What do you think?"

Magg almost laughed, "Jarrone, that would be so perfect! Let me know what you decide to do."

"I will do that."

It was decided that the wedding would be held in the village square where more people could come and celebrate together. It would be like the last celebration with dancing and lots of food for all. Zarcon had asked Donavan to perform the ceremony. Donavan was proud to do so. Things were coming along very nicely.

Meanwhile, Zarcon and Greta were happy to be together and bask in the love they felt for each other. Neither of them thought they could possibly be as happy as they were right then. Finally, their love would be recognized by everyone.

Greta in particular was having a hard time realizing that it was all real. Just the day before, she had been trying to adjust to the reality that Zarcon was dying. She had been so devastated then. Now, she was so unbelievably happy. She owed it all to Jarrone who hadn't given up on Zarcon and found a way to heal him. This was going to be a wonderful year after all and she would spend it with Zarcon and all their friends.

Magg and Jasmine were busy deciding on the decorations and what they would do to make a beautiful place for Zarcon and Greta to take their vows. It would have to be special for the two of them. They had waited so very long to finally get married.

Magg said, "I'm thinking we need to have some kind of arch with flowers on it where they will be married. What do you think, Jasmine?"

Jasmine thought about her wedding and how it was presented. "I think that's a great idea. Maybe we could make a path to the arch for Greta. Maybe flowers on both sides of the path or something else that would be pretty. Can you think of a way to do that?"

"Jasmine, I kind of think that Jarrone would love to come up with something. Maybe we could even have Revinia make a wedding dress for Greta."

Jasmine got excited about that, "Magg, what a great idea! That way both of them can do a lot to make it a wonderful experience. Jarrone already offered to make fireworks, right?"

"Yes, he did. He is so powerful! And if he doesn't know how to do something, he finds a way to do it. He's so creative and learns so fast. Let's go talk to both of them right now."

So, it was that Magg and Jasmine walked to the home of Jarrone and his family.

Magg knocked on the door and they waited for someone to answer.

Jarrone finally came to the door and smiled when he saw them both looking excited about something. He almost felt concern because he knew it would be something they wanted him to do.

He said, "It's good to see the both of you. What's going on?"

Magg laughed, "Jarrone, why would you say that? We just came for a visit."

Jarrone didn't believe that for one minute. "Really? Well, come on in and let's talk."

Jasmine spoke up, "Would you mind asking Revinia to join us?"

"Of course, I'll go find her right now." He walked into the next room and hollered up the stairs, "Revinia, come join the guests please. They want to talk to both of us."

Revinia came running down the stairs to see what was going on. "What is it, Jarrone?"

"Magg and Jasmine are here. I really don't know why, but I can guess." He was smiling when he said the last.

When Revinia walked into the room, Magg and Jasmine stood and gave her a hug.

Magg said "Revinia, it is so good to see you. You are prettier every day."

Revinia blushed and said, "Well, thank you. Now, tell me what's going on."

Magg laughed, "We can't hide anything, can we? Alright, Jasmine and I would like to talk to both you and Jarrone about help with the wedding coming up soon. Jarrone told you about Zarcon and Greta, right?"

"He did and I'm so excited that he was able to cure Zarcon. He worked really hard on that spell. Will you tell us what you need or want from us?"

Jasmine took a turn explaining, "We wondered, Revinia, if you would like to make Greta's wedding dress."

Revinia almost fainted from joy. "Really? I would love to! How much time will I have to make it?"

Magg cleared her throat, "Um, probably five days. Is that even possible? Zarcon is getting better really fast and they want to be married as soon as possible."

Again, Revinia nearly fainted, "Five days?? You'll bring me the fabric today, right? I'll need to get started by tonight if it's going to be done in just five days' time."

Magg stammered, "Well, um, yes, um, we'll get it by dinner time today, maybe sooner. Will that be soon enough?" She was hoping they would indeed be able to find something beautiful on this day. But she was concerned that maybe it would be difficult.

Next, Jarrone spoke up, "You said you wanted to talk to both of us. What is it that you want from me?"

Jasmine was excited to talk to him about what she and Magg had been talking about.

"Jarrone, you said you wanted to help with the planning, right? We were wondering if maybe you could create a pathway to an arch we are going to build for the ceremony. If you could make it pretty somehow, that would be wonderful. What do you think?"

Jarrone decided to make them squirm a bit, "Well, let me think about that. You're asking a lot, you know. I've never done anything like that before. It sounds really difficult." In his heart, he was glad for the chance to do something wonderful for Greta and Zarcon.

Magg was getting anxious, "Like healing Zarcon was a walk in the park, right?"

Jarrone laughed. They knew then that Jarrone had been having fun with them. They both laughed when they realized what he was doing.

"So, what do you think Jarrone?" They said together.

"I think that it would be one of few things I can have fun with. I will do it and have a great time doing it. Just let me know where it's to be and how long."

Magg smiled and was truly happy, "Jarrone, you really are the greatest. We can show you what we're thinking whenever you're ready to start."

Jarrone smiled, "How about tomorrow morning? You'll be busy finding fabric today."

"Sounds good, Jarrone. We'll be ready tomorrow. Meet us in the village square in the morning."

At that, they both bid their farewells and headed for the village store to find some special fabric for Greta's dress. As they walked toward town, they talked about all that needed to be done and the gratitude they felt that they had such talented young people to help them.

As they entered the village store, Jasmine spoke up, "Hello, as you know there's a wedding for Zarcon and Greta in a few days. We would like to see any fabric that would work for a wedding dress for Greta."

There were two young people to help them. They pulled down three fabrics that they thought might work. One was a lavender silk, one was a pale yellow brocade, and the last one was a deep blue velvet. Both Magg and Jasmine knew that Greta loved the color blue. So they picked the blue velvet for her dress. It was beautiful and would look so great on Greta's slender figure. They ordered how much they needed and when it was ready, they happily paid for it and left the shop.

Magg and Jasmine were so excited to have found such beautiful fabric in the small store in the village. It was almost unbelievable. They happily walked up to Jarrone's family home and knocked on the door.

Revinia opened the door with a big smile on her face. "Did you find something that will make a pretty dress for Greta?"

"Oh, Revinia, we sure did." Magg took the velvet out of the bag and showed Revinia. Revinia gasped at how beautiful it was.

She said, "Magg, this is so pretty! It will make a beautiful dress. I can hardly wait to get started!"

Magg smiled at that and said, "In your hands it will be. We can't wait to see what you create!"

All were smiles as they hugged Revinia and said their goodbyes. It had been a very good day.

As they were walking back to the inn, Matton came walking up to Magg and took her hand and said, "I've missed you. May I walk with you back to your room, milady? Magg just giggled.

Jasmine was so happy for her friend Magg. She had found so much love with Matton. Jasmine was thinking maybe there would be another wedding before very much time passed. It made her happy to think of it.

The three of them walked to the inn and went their separate ways. Donavan met Jasmine at the door of their room with a sly smile on his face that meant only one thing to them both. So much love in the air it couldn't be helped.

~

When morning came, Jarrone was waiting for Magg and Jasmine to show him where they wanted the path to the arch and where the ceremony would take place. The two women came out of the inn just in time. Jasmine guided Jarrone to the place where the path should start and where it would end. There would be people on both sides of the path cheering Greta on as she walked toward Zarcon. Jarrone could imagine how it would be. He was excited to start planning what it would look like.

He said, "Jasmine, I think this is going to be more fun than I thought. I'm already thinking about the flowers and slate for the path. This will be beautiful for Greta and Zarcon. Have you got the arch ready yet?"

Jasmine turned red, "Well, not just yet. I'm not really sure how to make one. Maybe you and Magg could come up with something pretty. What do you think, Magg?"

Magg looked at Jarrone and said, "We can do it for sure. Right, Jarrone?"

"Right. Can we talk about it now?"

Magg thought for a moment, "I think it would be a good idea to talk about it now, since the wedding is to be in four days. What are you thinking? I would like to make one out of wood and cover it with the same flowers you'll be using for the path. Or we could create a vine of some kind to cover it. What do you think?"

Jarrone smiled, "I think the same way. Only I like the vine idea the best. Is there someone in the village good with wood that can make an arch for us in a hurry? So we wouldn't have to build it ourselves."

Jasmine spoke up, "There is a man in the village that is an excellent carpenter. He has made some really great furniture for some of the villagers. His name is Theon. Want to go talk to him now?"

Magg said, "I think I'll wait until you two come back. You can tell me how it went then."

Jasmine agreed, so did Jarrone.

They walked to the carpenter's shop and walked in. Theon was at the front desk talking with one of the villagers. When he finished and she left, they walked up to the counter.

Jarrone said, "Theon, we were wondering if you would build an arch for the wedding to be held in four days. I know this is a short notice, but we just thought of it."

Theon laughed, "Four days to build an arch? How big?"

Jasmine said, "It needs to be about six feet high and three feet wide. We'll put vines on it to cover it with flowers. What do you think, Theon, can it be done?"

Theon laughed again, "It surely can! Arches are my specialty. I'll have it ready by tomorrow morning. Come to my shop before noon and let me know if you like it."

Jarrone was surprised, "Theon, that's amazing! It will be good to see what you can do."

Theon laughed again, "The truth is, I happen to have one that hasn't sold in the back. Would you like to see it now?"

Both said, "YES!"

So, they followed Theon to his back room and saw his arch up against the wall. It was the perfect size and would do nicely for the wedding. It had cross bars all along the middle of the arch, top to bottom. It would be great for the vines to cling to.

"This is perfect, Theon. Can we pick it up tomorrow morning like you said?" said Jarrone.

"Of course."

As they left the shop, they were both so happy to have found Theon and his wonderful arch all ready to go.

They walked up to Jarrone's cottage to see how Revinia was doing with the dress she was making for Greta.

They walked in and found Revinia working on the dress. Revinia held up what she had done so far. It was so beautiful that Jasmine had tears in her eyes. "This is going to be such a beautiful dress for Greta. I can't wait to see her face when it's finished. You are truly amazing, Revinia. I swear you have magic to do such wonderful things with a bit of fabric."

Revinia blushed, "Thank you, Jasmine. I've been wondering if maybe it was magic that helped me sew and create these dresses. I so enjoy creating them."

"It shows, my dear."

Revinia asked Jasmine if she could help with Greta's hair on the day of the wedding. Greta would be coming to try on the dress anyway and might as well get her hair done at the same time.

Jasmine was so happy that Revinia had offered to do Greta's hair. She hugged Revinia and told her it would be wonderful for her to do so. Jasmine then went back to the inn to tell Magg and Donavan what she had learned.

Jasmine walked to Magg's room and knocked. Magg answered with a smile. "What did you find out?"

Jasmine was so happy to report to Magg, "We talked with Theon and it turns out he had an arch that didn't sell and it's perfect. So we get to pick it up in the morning. Also, I went with Jarrone to his cottage and talked to Revinia about the dress. Oh, Magg! It's going to be fantastic. Greta will look like a queen in it. She told me it would be done in three days and ready before the wedding so Greta could try it on first. She also offered to help Greta with her hair."

Magg said, "It makes me so happy to hear that things are moving along so nicely. I'm also excited to work with Jarrone on the path and flowers. I'm glad we decided to use vines for the arch. Flowers are some of the favorite things I love to create. I'm sure that between Jarrone and me, we will make something amazing for Zarcon and Greta."

Jasmine agreed, "I for one am very excited to see what the two of you come up with. I'm sure everyone will be impressed. Most of all, Zarcon and Greta will be very happy to see everything we are doing for them. Just think! It's only three more days 'til the wedding."

~

Jarrone was busy laying the slate path for Greta. It was turning out to be very nice. After he got the path made, he went to find Magg so they could start putting the flowers on the sides of the path. Magg came out of the inn just as Jarrone was finishing up with the slate.

She said, "Jarrone, you've done a fantastic job with the path! The colors are amazing! Have you thought about what kind of flowers we should use?"

Jarrone answered, "I was thinking we could use something colorful. Do you have any ideas?"

Magg had been thinking about what to use so she suggested a rare flower from Synkana that she had seen as they left the city to fight the mist monsters. She described them to Jarrone and he tried to create the flower she described. He was close, but not quite right. So Magg tried to show him what she was thinking. This time it was perfect. Jarrone was impressed. The flowers really were colorful and just the right size for the path.

Now that they had decided to use those flowers, they both got to work lining the path with them. It turned out perfect and so lovely. Some of the villagers were watching what the two of them were doing and expressed their love of the result.

Jarrone was working on the arch. Jasmine had helped him bring it and put it in place the day before. He was able to set the arch so that it wouldn't blow or tip over. He used a quick spell to set it firmly in the ground.

Magg came to help him lace the flowered vines on the arch. They covered it with pretty blue flowers in Greta's honor. Blue flowers are not natural, but with magic, anything is possible.

The two of them were having a great time working together. And now their job was finished. The village square was almost ready for the wedding.

$\sim$

It was finally the day of the wedding. Greta and Zarcon were very ready to be married after all their years together. Now that they had professed their love to each other, they couldn't be parted. Greta was ready to meet with Revinia to try on her wedding dress and have her hair done for the wedding. She was so excited to see her dress.

Revinia and Jarrone brought Greta's dress to the inn very carefully. The velvet was somewhat delicate. Jarrone knocked on the door to Zarcon and Greta's door. Greta opened the door with a big smile on her face. She said, "Oh, Revinia, I'm so excited to see the dress you've made for me."

Revinia set the wrapped dress on the table and let Greta open the package.

As soon as she saw the color of the dress and that is to velvet, she gasped. "This is so beautiful!"

When she got the dress out of the wrapping, she started to cry. She stood back from the dress because water was not good for velvet. She mopped up her face and picked up the dress.

"Revinia! I'm beyond words! Zarcon, don't come in here. It's my wedding dress and you can't see it until the wedding. Let me try it on quick." Revinia helped Greta out of her house dress and lowered the new dress over her head. Once it was in place, it was perfect. Greta looked gorgeous. The blue matched her eyes and the dress made her look so slim and emphasized her curves.

Revinia started working on Greta's hair. It was long and thick and Revinia wound it around her head with small braids and ribbons to match her dress.

Jarrone had waited outside the door and came in when Revinia opened it so he could see what Greta looked like in her new dress.

Jarrone said, "Greta, I'm afraid you might be more beautiful than Zarcon can deal with. I'm so impressed with how you look in that dress. Revinia sewed on it for four solid days to have it ready for your wedding. I must say, Revinia, it was worth it. Look at Greta now! All I can say is, wow!"

Greta was embarrassed by Jarrone's compliment. She wasn't used to that kind of praise. But she loved it. She was now ready for the wedding.

The villagers were gathering in the village square to witness the wedding of Zarcon and Greta. The village band was playing some soft music as Zarcon and Donavan waited near the arch. Magg and Jasmine accompanied Greta to the path. When the villagers saw Greta, they gasped at how beautiful she was. Zarcon almost fell over in wonder at how beautiful she looked in her new dress. Donavan was stunned.

Greta walked up to Zarcon and kissed him lightly. Donavan began the ceremony saying,

"We are here today to witness the marriage of Zarcon and Greta. These two have known each other for many years and have finally decided to seal their love with marriage. Personally, I'm beyond words at how happy I am for the two of you. It's a miracle that we are here for this joyous occasion. Zarcon is healed and will continue to live with us for a long time yet. Greta has been by his side throughout his life and has supported him no matter what they faced. We honor them this day and wish them many years of joy together.

"Greta, do you take Zarcon to be your husband, to love and to cherish as long as you both shall live?"

"I most surely do, with all my heart."

"Zarcon, do you take Greta as your wife, to love and to cherish as long as you both shall live?" Zarcon was beside him with pride for Greta, "I most certainly do."

"I now pronounce you man and wife."

Everyone cheered at that while Zarcon and Greta kissed and then walked down the path to the inn where the celebration was about to begin.

Aribon had prepared a spectacular feast for all. Zarcon and Greta sat at the head of a very long table while everyone came in to eat and celebrate their marriage. Donavan and Jasmine sat on one side and Magg and Matton sat on the other side. Jarrone, Revinia, Lucintha, Hoskins, and their father sat next to Magg and Matton. The villagers filled in and sat with them. There was plenty of room for all those who could come. The food was the best ever.

Zarcon and Greta hardly had time to talk to each other. The villagers and friends were congratulating them one after another. Yet, in the back of their minds was the fact that none of this would have been possible without Jarrone and his magic. He had saved Zarcon at the very end of his life. Life was full of surprises.

As the meal wound down, and the villagers began to leave, it was soon time for dancing. Everyone went home to change into their dancing shoes and comfortable clothes. The celebration was not over yet.

There were naps to be had so they would be rested up for the dancing. Even Zarcon and Greta went to their room to rest up. They may not dance many dances, but it was their wedding and they wanted to celebrate too.

Magg and Matton went to Magg's room and tried to rest, but it didn't happen.

Donavan and Jasmine did the same. Weddings can have that effect on some people.

It was about two hours later that the band started playing dance music, luring everyone to come and dance. It was a beautiful night with a full moon and stars shining bright. There were torches set around the area to provide light. The villagers and friends started arriving. It was customary for the bride and groom to dance the first dance. They went along and kind of moved to the music. Everyone applauded and cheered. When the dance was over, they left the party and went to Zarcon's room for the night. It was obvious they would be cuddling and kissing.

Gradually, the others decided to dance too. The music was inviting and there was definitely love in the air. Revinia was dancing with her new boyfriend, Ricken. Lucintha found Alfias and asked him to dance. Jarrone was lost, not really knowing what to do. Then one of the prettiest girls in the village walked right up to him and asked him to dance. Jarrone was a bit shocked, but more than happy to dance with her.

Jarrone's father asked the widow, Marion, to dance. She was slim and attractive and he was really happy dancing with her. She seemed genuinely interested in him. Time would tell if it would go anywhere. They had gotten to know each other a bit at the party.

Hoskins, Jarrone's brother, danced a few times with the adults. Then a young girl walked up to him and asked him to dance. It was obvious that he was embarrassed. It had never happened before. But he danced with her and had a lot of fun.

Gradually, people started to go back home. It was getting late and the excitement had worn many of them out. Greta and Zarcon had gone to their room early in the evening. So, Magg and Matton, and Donavan and Jasmine decided to call it a night as well.

Jarrone and the other young people were still having a great time. Jarrone's father was worn out and invited his children to come home with him. There was a bit of complaint, but they didn't want him to go home alone. It was dark and things were quieting down. The band was giving up too. It had been a long day.

Revinia's boyfriend walked her home. Jarrone walked his new friend home. Lucintha said goodbye to Alfias and walked with her family. Hoskins was already home. He enjoyed dancing, but he was tired and decided to get home early.

Revinia spoke to her boyfriend, Ricken, "Thank you for dancing with me. I had a wonderful time."

Ricken replied, "I did too. It was great to be able to dance with you, Revinia. We had so much fun together."

They walked on quietly to Revinia's home. Ricken asked, "Can I see you again? Maybe we could go on a picnic soon. Does that sound fun?"

Revinia said, "It does, Ricken. Let's plan something like that in a couple of days."

Ricken gave Revinia a quick kiss and walked home.

Jarron saw the kiss and as they were walking into the cottage, he said, "I saw that kiss. I'm really glad it was quick. Anything else and I might have had to say something. He seems to be pretty honorable to me. How do you feel about him, Revinia?"

"Jarrone, I like him a lot, but it's nothing serious. I'm still more interested in magic."

"Good."

As they walked into the cottage, they heard a loud growling noise in the forest. They hurried inside, barred the door, and locked the window shutters. Whatever it was, it wasn't anything good.

The other villagers heard it too. Magg and Matton moved closer together. Donavan and Jasmine did the same. Zarcon and Greta were asleep in each other's arms.

CHAPTER 31

SOLVIG

BOREN AND KEDRON were so happy to be back in Solvig with Karmine and Roslin and their two sons, Mika and Lorin. They were happier than they had ever been. They felt safe and loved as part of the family. The only thing that bothered them was the fact that they really wanted to go to Anakik and see Zarcon.

They didn't say anything to Karmine or Roslin for a few days. Then, finally, they asked to talk to both of them for a few minutes.

Roslin said, "I think I know what this is about. You want to get to Anakik and see Zarcon, don't you?"

Kedron replied, "Yes, we really want to meet him and ask him about our magic, if we have any. Would that be possible?"

Karmine smiled, "I was wondering when you would ask that question. We decided that when you're ready to go, we'd like to go with you. Would that be alright with you two?"

They both shouted, "YES!"

So, they started planning their trip and what they would need and how long they could be gone. It was going to be so exciting to finally meet Zarcon and his friends. They had heard so much about them.

Anakik was a day's ride from Solvig. They decided to use the wagon so they could all ride together. They would spend two weeks there and get to know the people and especially Zarcon. Maybe he would test them to see if they had any magic and go from there. It was so exciting for them. They could hardly wait to go.

As preparations were made, the excitement grew. They packed up enough food to last their time on the road and their clothes were being cleaned and packed. Roslin was busy cooking and packing their food. It was mostly sandwiches and water. She also baked some cookies that the boys loved. So much to do to leave the next day.

In the morning, they got out of bed early, ate a quick breakfast, and loaded the wagon to leave. The boys made a lot of noise in their excitement. Mika and Lorin were almost as excited as Boren and Kedron. When all was ready, they were ordered onto the back of the wagon while Karmine and Roslin rode in the front. The horses were ready and sensed the excitement of the others. They were a bit restive.

Finally, they were off and out of Solvig headed for Anakik. They took the main road with the wagon. The trail was just too narrow and rough. They sang songs and laughed and chatted the entire day's ride. They stopped once to eat some lunch and relax themselves and the horses. It was a beautiful day with the sun shining and birds singing in the trees. They saw a deer on the other side of the road eating grass and ignoring them. Such a wonderful day for all of them.

They reluctantly packed the wagon and were ready to move on. As they got into the wagon and Karmine started the horses moving, they hadn't gone very far when they noticed a large animal moving toward them at a fast pace. Karmine snapped his whip and got the horses running as fast as possible.

The animal kept up with them and appeared to be gaining on them. Luckily, Karmine had brought his big rifle for just such an emergency. He gave Roslin the reins and got his rifle out from under the seat, ready to shoot if necessary.

It was difficult to steady the gun while being in the moving wagon, but Karmine did his best. The boys sensed the danger and could see the animal moving alongside the road after them. They tried not to cry, but they were really scared.

They were approaching Anakik swiftly at this point. They were almost there. The animal was getting too close for comfort so Karmine had to try to shoot it. He fired his rifle at the monster and hit it in the side, but he kept coming.

The sound of the rifle shot alerted the people in Anakik. Magg and Donavan came running to see what was happening. Just then, they could see the wagon coming and a large animal about to drag one of the boys out of it.

Magg saw the danger and began a spell to stop it. She let the spell go toward the monster and prayed it would do the trick to stop it. It hit the thing and it fell backward taking the boy with it. Magg ran toward the monster to save the boy. She threw a spell at it that caused its head to explode. It twitched and held onto the boy until it finally died. The boy was scared half to death thinking he was going to die right then. He could hardly believe he survived. He had been saved, but he was bloody from the monster's head being blown up.

Kedron looked up and saw Magg standing over him about to pick him up and check him over. He was shaking and crying. Roslin came to him and took him from Magg, "Oh, thank you for saving my son. I was sure he would be dead right then. You came just in time." Roslin was crying too. Karmine jumped down from the wagon to see if Kedron was alright, then he couldn't help himself and gave Magg a big hug. "Thank you, thank you, thank you! You can't imagine what this boy has been through in his short life. This is almost more than any of us can bear."

Donavan came up beside Magg and was once again amazed at Magg's quick action to save the boy. As he was looking at the monster, he realized it was like the one she had cremated when they were going back to Anakik after destroying the mist monsters.

He said softly, "Magg, do you see what I see?"

"I do, indeed. This is the same kind of animal that attacked us before. The one I burned, right?"

"It sure is. Now we know there are more of them. I was afraid of this."

Karmine overheard them, "What are you talking about? You mean there are more of these awful things around here?"

Donavan answered, "It appears so. I believe it's something new. We have been here for quite some time and haven't seen them until recently. I'm so glad you came this way, just in time for us to help."

Karmine sighed, "We were headed this way because the boy you saved, Kedron, and his brother Boren wanted to meet Zarcon and spend time with him and his friends. Do you know where we might find them?"

Magg smiled, "Yes, in fact, the two of us are part of that group. Zarcon is living at the village inn and will be so happy to meet you all. Did you ever see Neberon? He almost killed Zarcon. He would have succeeded, but our new wizard, Jarrone, healed him with a new spell he created. Neberon did some damage near here. It was the small village of Solvig. Do you know the place?"

Karmine said, "We just came from Solvig. We live there. We did see Neberon as he went through our village looking for Jarrone. Is it the same Jarrone we know? What an amazing young man he is! This is amazing! And now the boys can meet Zarcon and find out what magic they might have."

Magg spoke up, "Zarcon will be glad to do that. It also happens that we're planning on starting a school for anyone with magic, big or small. In fact, the construction of the school should be finished in another three months. That should also give him something to look forward to."

"We'll tell him that, and that he will actually get to meet Zarcon."

Roslin called Kedron and Boren over to her and Magg. It would be fun to see their reaction in getting to meet Zarcon and learning about the school.

"Kedron and Boren, please come here and let's talk about Zarcon and something special. Magg will tell you about it."

"Hello, boys, my name is Magg, as you know. I'm so glad I was able to help you with that monster. I'm afraid there are more of them. So we have to be very careful when going anywhere. Zarcon is well and living in Anakik. So you will able to meet him. There is something else you'll be happy to know about. We're building a new school that will be finished in a few months. It's for anyone who has magic and we want to help them learn about how to use it and discover what kind of magic they might have. What do you think? Would you like to come to the school?"

Both boys said, "Oh, yes. That's what we've been waiting for so long."

"Did you ever see Neberon?"

"We sure did. He killed our families."

"I'm so sorry. That must have been horrible. I want to hear about it when we get back to Anakik."

Magg continued, "Well, in the battle with Neberon here in Anakik, Zarcon was hit in the arm by one of Neberon's spells. It was red glass that was poisoned. It's actually what hurt Zarcon so bad that he got really sick, and after awhile it looked like he might die. But, you know Jarrone, I'm told. Well, he created a spelll that was able to heal Zarcon. It was a miracle for sure."

Kedron smiled and said, "Will we really get to meet Zarcon? He's really doing well? Jarrone healed him? We've been wanting to meet him for months. It's what has kept us going since Neberon killed our families. I'm so excited and we're nearly there."

Roslin came closer to Kedron and gave him a big hug, "I'm so glad you will meet Zarcon. This is an exciting day indeed."

Magg added, "You will also meet the friends of Zarcon and learn from them. There are two especially who have been with Zarcon for a long time. Donavan is one of them. And there's one woman who loved him dearly for years. They got married just a few days ago. You will love them. The school will start soon and you will learn so much about magic. You'll get to see Zarcon's book of magic that includes the history of magic too."

Kedron was so happy at that. He wanted to stay in Anakik awhile and meet Zarcon's friends and learn from them. He really wanted to meet Zarcon, too. He said, "I'm pretty sure this is what I want to do."

Kedron looked at Roslin and Karmine, "Would it be alright if we stay awhile?"

Karmine replied, "Kedron, if it's what you want to do, it's alright. We can stay as long as you like."

Magg smiled, "Kedron, whatever you want to do will be fine. We'll find a place for you and your family that will give you time to decide how you feel about everything we discussed."

Kedron looked to Boren for reasurance. Boren was happy, too, and he was able to give Kedron a sign of approval. Roslin and Karmine were also willing to go along with the plan. They wanted to help Kedron and Boren in whatever they needed to do now that they were close to Anakik and Zarcon and his friends.

Roslin said, "Can we follow you, Magg, to Anakik and where we will be able to stay? And what are we going to do about this terrible monster? He needs burying at least."

Magg smiled again, "I have a method to get rid of its body. I'll show you if you want to watch."

The boys spoke up, "We do!"

So Magg started her cremation spell right then. As the family watched her, she sent her spell into the monster and burned it to ashes.

"Wow!! That was so amazing! I want to learn how to do that! Will you teach us that at the school?"

"It will take a long time to learn enough to do it, but when you're ready, I will teach you."

"Hooray!"

Donavan was grateful that Magg was able to talk to the boys. He said, "Boys, I would like to guide you into Anakik and present you and your family to Zarcon and his friends. What do you say?"

The family was very excited to go the rest of the way to Anakik and start a new chapter in their lives.

CHAPTER 32

ANAKIK AT LAST

AS THEY ENTERED Anakik, the boys were amazed at how big it was and how many people lived there. It was much larger than Solvig. There was much more to see and Donavan and Magg showed them around the village and the cottage in town that they would be staying in.

Roslin and Karmine were pleased with their cottage. The boys were happy to be close to the forest to play in during the day. There was an air of joy in the village because of Greta and Zarcon's wedding. The celebration had been really fun.

When Roslin and Karmine and the boys came into town in their wagon, everyone came to meet them and find out more about them. The people were very friendly and wanted to help if they needed any. It was so nice to see such friendly people.

Mika and Lorin were a bit overwhelmed by all of it. They didn't really understand what was happening. But they were excited to find out what it all meant. Mika was really glad that Kedron and Boren were happy.

As Roslin and the family got down from the wagon, Jasmine and Matton came to see what was going on and to find out what had happened on the road. They had heard the sound of the rifle firing and came out to see if they could help with anything.

Matton ran to Magg, "What happened? Is everyone alright?"

"Yes, everyone is fine, but I had to destroy another one of those monsters we saw on the way back to Anakik. It was going to attack this family when Donavan and I arrived to help. Do you remember how it was about to attack you?"

"I sure do. That's terrifying if there really are more of them. So, you burned it up like before?"

"I sure did. It was kind of fun too." They both laughed at that.

Others gathered around to hear the story. Magg was happy to tell them more about it.

Kedron spoke up, "And it was trying to eat me when Magg zapped it."

Everyone looked at Magg with renewed respect. Magg had arrived just in time from what Kedron was saying.

Jasmine had walked to Donavan and hugged him. She was glad he was alright. "So, who are these people, Donavan?"

"They were coming to meet Zarcon. Magg told them about what happened to him and how Jarrone healed him. She also invited them to join the school when it's ready. We brought them the rest of the way into Anakik to meet us and stay for a few days, maybe a couple of weeks. We showed them this cottage to stay in while they're here. They seem to like it. I'm so glad the school is nearly finished. It's something for the boys to look forward to."

"That sounds good. Maybe once they get settled in their cottage, we could invite them to dinner at the inn. That way they can meet all of us and we could get to know them too. What do you think?"

"I think it's a great idea. Greta and Zarcon will enjoy meeting them and finding out more about them."

"I know. I think it will be a nice time to celebrate and have some fun while they're here. I see the school is coming along nicely. It will be great when it's finally finished and we can start classes."

"I agree. We need to have that to distract the children and give them something to do besides running around screaming. Don't you think?"

"I surely do." They both were smiling as they said that last bit.

Roslin finally said, "We would surely appreciate getting settled into the cottage. After such a morning, I could use a nap and I'm sure Karmine and the boys feel the same."

The group around them apologized for keeping them so long and quietly went about their business. Magg and Jasmine stayed to help with the boys and get everything they would need into the cottage. Roslin had brought some linens for the beds, just in case, and the beds were made up and ready for napping in no time at all. The six of them were down and asleep before much time passed.

Magg and Jasmine were happy that they were all settled in. Jasmine told Magg about her plan to have them over for dinner at the inn later on. She readily agreed. She also felt that it would be a good thing for Greta and Zarcon to be with everyone and meet the new family.

Jasmine went to Aribon about dinner for everyone the next day. He was also excited to meet the new family. She then went to talk with Greta and Zarcon.

"Greta, I have a proposal for you and Zarcon. We have a new family here for a couple of weeks. So, to welcome them, we would like to have a dinner with everybody to meet them and they can also meet us and we can get to know each other a bit. Will you please come? It will be tomorrow night. We need you and Zarcon to meet them and let us know what you think."

"We would like that."

Jasmine left Greta and headed to meet Jarrone and his family. She wanted to be sure they were included in the dinner for Roslin and her family. She felt the more people that welcomed the family the better, and maybe they would decide to stay in Anakik.

She was getting close to Jarrone's cottage and noticed that Jarrone was taking care of the horses out at their barn. She walked up to him and said, "Hello, Jarrone. Are you busy or can we talk about something for just a few minutes?"

Jarrone was surprised to see Jasmine. He and his family were usually left alone most of the time. He said, "Well, hello, Jasmine. What brings you here to this end of town?"

"Well, we have a new family staying in one of the cottages in the middle of the village and we would like to have a dinner for them so they can meet all of us and get to know us a little. We also want to get to know them. They have four boys that maybe will join our school of magic. Can you and your family join us? It will be a wonderful dinner and it will get us out of our rooms for a few hours. It should be fun. What do you say?"

Jarrone was surprised again. He and his family had not been invited to anything since the wedding. He said, "Let me tell my family about it and get their opinion on the idea."

Jasmine was disappointed that he couldn't answer her right then. But she understood his need to consult his family to be sure they wanted to take part in it. So, she asked Jarrone to let her know his decision as soon as possible. She would be at the inn the rest of the day.

Jarrone was glad to be invited, but he wanted to know how family felt about it. He said goodbye to Jasmine and assured her he would let her know. He went to their cottage and spoke with his family about the dinner.

"Hey, everyone. I just spoke with Jasmine about a dinner tomorrow night that they're having for a new family in town. It will give us a chance to meet them and get to know them a bit while they get to know us too. What do you think, want to go?"

His two sisters, Revinia and Lucintha, were more than excited to go. Hoskins, his brother, was alright with it, but not excited. He was somewhat a loner currently. His father was glad to get out of the house and go do something different. So everyone was in agreement that they wanted to go. Jarrone let them know that he had to go tell Jasmine about it and that meant going to town, to the inn, to find her.

His sisters wanted to come too. So, they all three headed for the inn as evening was coming on. The walk wasn't far and the night was warm. It didn't take long to get to the inn and find Jasmine. She was happy to see the three of them.

"I'm so glad the three of you came to see me and tell me if you're coming to the dinner. Are you?"

Revinia spoke up, "We are! We're so excited to get to be a part of the dinner. We heard there was a new family in town, but we didn't see them. I guess they've only been here a day or so, right?"

"Right. They got here today as a matter of fact. They seem really nice."

Jarrone said, "I guess we'd better head back home. It's getting late and we have a lot to do tomorrow. See you tomorrow, Jasmine, and thanks for the invitation."

Jarrone and his sisters walked home happy to have been away for a few minutes. They got home just as the sun went down. Their father was waiting for them in his favorite chair with the blanket on his lap that he really liked. He wasn't being waited on like before, but that was alright with him. He felt better about doing things for himself now.

Hoskins had gone to bed. He'd worn himself out chasing woodland creatures all day. He was a strange boy. He did seem to have some magic starting at his age. He was nearly twelve and it was time for it to show up, if he had any that is. Only time would tell.

As a family, they were doing really well. Revinia had a boy she really liked and Lucintha was happy to not have a boyfriend just yet. Jarrone was still watching the boys who came courting Revinia. They seemed to be alright by his standard, at least so far. Jarrone didn't have a girlfriend and he really wanted one. Watching Revinia with her boyfriend made him feel a little lonely.

For now, they had the dinner to look forward to. He was so glad they had been invited.

~

Morning came and there was much to do for everyone to prepare for the dinner that night. Roslin and Karmine were getting things put away and organized in their cottage. The boys were excited to see who lived in Anakik. They hadn't met very many in the last day or so. Roslin was going to make sure the boys had a bath and clean clothes to wear. She prepared breakfast; eggs and bacon with some flapjacks to go with. Karmine and the four boys ate as if they hadn't eaten in a week. She loved that they ate so well. It would be a fun day for them all.

Jasmine and Donavan were getting things put together. The tables were set up with Aribon and Alfias' help. Magg and Matton took care of letting all the villagers know about it. They were invited, but many couldn't make it with so much to do of their own. It would still be a big dinner. So much to do in one day. But it would be great and the food would be too.

Jarrone and his sisters were deciding what to wear and to get their father ready. They had a late breakfast of eggs and ham with some berry juice. A bath was necessary for them all. That alone took a long time with heating the water on the stove and filling their metal bath tub.

Finally, they were getting ready. Hoskins was not happy to have to bathe. But he went along with it to avoid any fighting that might happen if he said he didn't want to. So he bathed and found some clean clothes to wear. It was a struggle for him, but he finally managed to be ready on time.

As the time to leave drew closer, they decided to walk down to the inn to help if needed. They got there in time to help with the table settings and centerpieces which were some autumn flowers in bowls. It was looking really nice.

Zarcon was dressed in his wizard robes and looked especially regal. Greta wore the dress Revinia had made for her. Greta was so grateful to be with him as his wife. They walked out to meet Magg and the others. They applauded the two of them. Zarcon and Greta looked almost royal.

All of them went to the dining room then. Those who were there were so surprised at how beautiful Greta looked and Zarcon was magnificent in his robes. Their friends could hardly believe it. They actually applauded when Zarcon and Greta walked in. Greta was so happy she nearly cried.

Jarrone was so glad they came. He was touched that Greta loved his sister's dress so much that she would wear it again for the party. Revinia really was very talented. She seemed to know exactly what would be the best for the person she sewed for. It had to be a form of magic.

A bit later Roslin and her family came into the inn. They were cheered by those in the dining area. Aribon and Alfias had prepared a wonderful meal for everyone. As they sat down to dinner, the chatter was pleasant and merry. Everyone wanted to find out all they could about Roslin and the family. Karmine was so happy to meet these kind people. He felt safe with his family there. The boys were happily eating their fill and talking with the other children. There were several families with children who sat close to them.

Roslin and Karmine were wondering if they would live in Anakik. It might be a really good thing for them and the boys. They would discuss it later when the boys were in bed.

Chatting with Jasmine and Donavan and Magg with Matton was so nice. Being friends with these wonderful people would be so great. They felt as though they already fit in. The boys were making new friends with each passing moment. The thought occurred to them that it might be difficult to get them to go back to Solvig. They would wait and see what happened before they had to leave. They would enjoy the next week or two while they were there and then decide.

CHAPTER 33

MAGIC SCHOOL

T HE SCHOOL FOR magic was being built on the outskirts of the
village. It was going to be really big because Magg and Donavan
were hoping for many students to come to learn magic. There would be
rooms for the students, a kitchen to prepare their meals, and a library
for the study of magic. There would also, of course, be classrooms and
laboratories for the students to practice the magic they were learning.

The villagers were excited to help build the school since some of their
own children would be attending, it was hoped. Jarrone was involved in
the design and building of the school. He seemed to have a natural talent
for such things. He was growing in maturity and Magg and Donavan
were happy to see it. He would be a fine wizard in time.

As Karmine and Roslin watched the school coming together, they
were anxious for the boys to see how it was going. When Roslin mentioned
going to check out the school, the boys were so excited they could hardly
sit still. Boren and Kedron wanted to attend that school in order to see
what kind of magic they might have. Roslin's two boys thought that maybe
they might have some magic too. So, they a packed lunch and went for
the short hike to see the school.

The path to the school was already well-marked. When they rounded a turn in the path, they all gasped. The school was much closer to being completed than they thought it might be. The boys ran to see it up close. There was no door on the front just yet, but inside, it was looking nearly finished. It was going to be beautiful.

Jarrone met the boys at the doorway and invited them in.

"Come on in, boys. What do you think? Are you about ready to start school?"

Kedron was almost jumping up and down in excitement. "You bet! We can hardly wait to start."

Jarrone thought for a minute then said, "How would you like to help me paint some of the rooms?"

The boys were eager and said all at once, "Please, may we?"

"I would really like it if you did. It would be so nice to have students involved with finishing the school. You can help paint the rooms for the kids. If you decide to add some artwork, just tell me what you want to do, and maybe you can do it. Will you think about what you would like to do and let me know? We'll be ready to paint in about a week."

Karmine and Roslin were so excited to see the boys have the opportunity to paint and maybe even add some artwork to the children's rooms. It was getting harder and harder to think of moving back to Solvig. They knew the boys would not be happy to leave Anakik now. Maybe that was what they needed to do, move to Anakik permanently. Something to think about.

After the tour of the school, they decided to sit on the rocks just outside the school and have lunch. It was a cool afternoon with the sun shining, but it was getting close to autumn and there was a bit of a chill in the air. There was also a stream nearby that sang to them as they ate. The green forest was turning to reds and yellows as the year moved on.

Lunch was great and the tour of the school was wonderful. Now, they could hardly wait to start. This would be a good thing for the boys, they were sure. Karmine and the boys helped Roslin pick up the lunch things and put them in the bag to take back to their cottage. They had been discussing the school and how long it might be before the boys could start. Getting invited to help paint the rooms had been a wonderful idea. It would be really fun to start that too.

So much to think about. Karmine and Roslin decided to wait to talk to the boys about staying in Anakik. They had enough excitement to last them a while. Life just kept getting more and more interesting.

Meanwhile, Magg and Matton were together in Magg's room. Magg was talking about the school and what they might teach the students. The planning was getting nowhere, so Magg decided it would be a good time to get Zarcon, Jasmine, Donavan, and Jarrone involved. It was their school too. Magg was the head of the school, but she didn't feel like she should make all the decisions. She invited the rest of the group to meet in the dining room of the inn where there were tables and paper to write on.

When the rest of the group came in, Magg asked them to sit at the tables and be ready to discuss the school and what exactly they would teach. It wasn't just about magic, there would be math classes, language, and reading. They wanted the students, no matter their age, to be able to think for themselves and be able to express themselves on paper. They would also learn the history of magic and how it was used throughout time. There would also be strict rules for behavior and the use of magic. It was hoped that they could avoid creating someone like Neberon. They would be vigilant for the presence of any evil in the school and stop it as soon as may be.

The group decided who would teach which subject and how long it would be taught. It was exciting to think they were so close to starting the school. It had taken so long to build, and now they were actually getting the classes lined up to start in a few weeks.

Jarrone told them about having the boys paint the rooms for the children and how they might paint some artwork on the walls to make it fun. Jasmine and Magg were so happy that Jarrone had taken the initiative to do such a fun thing. Jarrone told them how excited the boys had been to get started.

It was also discussed that the new family might decide to stay in Anakik. It was looking more and more like that would make more sense than driving their wagon back and forth to Solvig. But the family would decide on their own.

CHAPTER 34

SCHOOL BEGINS

T HE SCHOOL WAS nearly finished and those wishing to attend were becoming more and more anxious to start classes. Boren and Kedron were especially excited. They were going to learn what magic they might have. Kedron seemed to be the one with the most potential. But both boys had parents with magic. It would be fun to find out what their magic might be.

As the people of the village completed the finishing touches, the school was beginning to look wonderful. The children of the village had been given the opportunity to paint their own art on the classroom walls that they would be using. It was looking really fun. The rest of the school was painted in bright colors except red. It was known that red brought out the anger in certain individuals, especially if they had magic.

The floors were being finished in wood from the forest. The oak and walnut trees made wonderful flooring. Some of the villagers knew how to make ceramic tiles and those were used in the laboratories that would be used for magic. There would also be classes in biology and the use of herbs to cure.

It was decided that school would start on the first of the very next month. Those teaching magic knew what they wanted to do and how to start. Teaching things besides magic were also prepared. The classes and room assignments were made and agreed upon. All that was needed now were the students. It looked like there would be plenty of those as well.

Zarcon would be involved in teaching if he was needed. He was recovered from the poison of Neberon's glass, but needed time to be with his new bride, Greta. Their wedding had been wonderful. Everyone was so happy for them that many tears of joy were shed.

Zarcon and Greta acted like a young couple with smiles and giggles throughout the day. They spent a good deal of time being affectionate. It didn't seem possible that the two were finally married. They had acted like friends for so many years, no one suspected that they loved each other more than friends. Life was like that sometimes.

Life in the village had become what it had always been before the mist monsters came. There was happiness and love and lots of fun for everyone.

Life in Anakik had quieted down and anticipation for the start of school was building. There was only a week left before it started.

It was a good thing they had thought ahead to build a place for the students from out of town to stay. There were many young people who had signed up for classes from as far away as Synkana. Families were bringing their children to the village to stay and needed rooms at the inn for themselves. For the first set of classes, it looked like they might need to add on to the school soon.

Zarcon was so glad he was still alive and able to participate in the school, and to finally have his precious Greta as his wife. Jarrone had done something unbelievable and Zarcon was grateful that he was the one to receive that gift of life. He had truly thought his life to be over until Jarrone entered his room that fateful day. He now felt better than he had in years.

CHAPTER 35

MAGIC

A S THE SUN was coming up over the mountains, Jarrone was meeting Magg and Donavan to learn a new powerful spell that would destroy the creatures that had started scaring them, at night especially. Magg had been able to destroy two of them with a particular spell and she was going to teach Jarrone and Donavan how to do it.

"Good morning! Did either of you hear the loud roar last night?" asked Magg.

Jarrone replied, "We sure did. We had just gone to bed when we heard it."

Donavan said, "Jasmine and I were just getting ready to go to bed when we heard it."

Magg said, "It looks like we're just in time to learn my spell so we will be ready when it comes into our village to do harm. Let me show you how it goes."

The three of them worked on mastering the spell all morning. At lunchtime, they decided to stop and go to the inn for food. They were all sweating and tired anyway and needed the rest. Jarrone was feeling happy with his progress, as was Donavan. Both of them nearly had the spell mastered. It seemed to be just in time.

The new monsters were moving in and the group of wizards must be ready to fight them before there were too many of them to succeed.

What would they do if that happened? Would it be like the mist monsters all over again? The thought was not to be born just now. They were preparing the best they could before it was necessary to fight.

In the meantime, they would enjoy this quiet time together. Starting the school, with all the details involved, would be enough for now. Trouble would come in its own time. At least they had each other to depend on to get through whatever that might mean for the future.

Milton Keynes UK
Ingram Content Group UK Ltd.
UKHW010640040324
438885UK00001B/177